EXERCISE IS MURDER

A Smiley and McBlythe Mystery

Exercise Is Murder

Published by Jubilee Publishing, LLC
Paperback ISBN 978-1-958252-19-2

Cover design: Streetlight Graphics
Editors:
Teresa Lynn, Tranquility Press
Kit Duncan

EXERCISE IS MURDER

A Smiley and McBlythe Mystery

BRUCE HAMMACK

Also by Bruce Hammack

The Smiley and McBlythe Mystery Series

Exercise Is Murder, Prequel

Jingle Bells, Rifle Shells,

Pistols And Poinsettias

Five Card Murder

Murder In The Dunes

The Name Game Murder

Murder Down The Line

Vision Of Murder

Mistletoe, Malice And Murder

A Beach To Die For

Dig Deep For Murder

The Star of Justice Series

Long Road To Justice

A Murder Redeemed

A Grave Secret

Justice On A Midnight Clear

The Fen Maguire Mystery Series

Murder On The Brazos

Murder On The Angelina

Murder On The Guadalupe

Murder On The Wichita

Murder On The San Gabriel

See my latest catalog of books at brucehammack.com/books.

1

Three firm knocks sounded on the classroom door.

"Enter." The command came from the instructor.

Heather McBlythe looked up from her desk at Houston's Police Academy, a sprawling complex spread over seventy acres, butting up to the southwest corner of George Bush International Airport. She found the location of the airport to be a noisy aggravation at first, but decided it was a good setting for learning to deal with frequent interruptions and the resulting stress.

A loud creak from a squeaking hinge interrupted the chatter of the room's occupants. Into the classroom walked a disheveled man, feeling his way with a white cane. The sweeping motions, like the slow wag of a dog's tail, came with a light tap and scrape. He stopped briefly as the instructor announced, "This is retired homicide detective Steve Smiley. You can see on your syllabus that he'll be teaching SKILLS OF OBSERVATION AND DEDUCTION. They're all yours, Steve."

Who could imagine that a blind former cop would be teaching at the Academy, let alone a class dealing with observation? A snicker came from the back of the room. Instead of speaking, the retired detective adjusted his sunglasses and used his cane to orient himself to the room. He felt his way around the front without speaking, his steps slow and balking. Most of the recruits sat in silence, watching the man shuffle until he had explored the front of the classroom. A muffled conversation rose from the rear of the room. When the former detective came to the wall nearest Heather, he turned and followed it until she felt the cane touch her foot.

"What's your name, young lady?" Smiley asked.

She rose to her feet. "Heather McBlythe, sir."

"Thank you, McBlythe. Please be seated."

The cane scraped the vinyl composition tile floor in back-and-forth searches as he made his way along the first row of seats toward the door of the classroom. Along the way he slowed as the metal tip, the approximate size of two nickels glued together, came in contact with one foot after another. At the last row before reaching the door he turned and shuffled down an aisle until he reached the rear wall. He backtracked and turned to the occupant in the last seat.

"What's your name, son?"

"Hank Strother... Hank Strother, sir."

"Don't bother standing, Hank."

Some of her classmates stifled a laugh while others straightened their posture. Heather covered a grin with her hand. She'd heard enough in the last few days from the yokel in the back row. He needed to be thrown back to whatever backwater he came from.

The mysterious former detective traversed his way back to the front of the classroom. Once there he pointed down the center aisle. "Fourth seat. What's your name?"

"Mary Bannon, sir," she said after she had risen to her feet.

"Tell me, Bannon, what do you know about the death of former District Attorney Ned Logan?"

"Uh... nothing, sir."

"Nothing? You haven't heard about it on TV or read about it? Are you telling me a former assistant district attorney is dead and you and your fellow recruits haven't been discussing it?"

She spoke in a weak, warbling voice. "Well, yeah. I mean, yes, sir. I overheard some of—"

"So you do know something about it. Is that what you're saying? Why didn't you tell me the truth the first time I asked you?"

The serrated edge of his words cut through the air and left Mary Bannon a stuttering mess. Heather tilted her head. There was more to the curmudgeon than she'd originally thought. Time to pay attention.

"I... I thought you meant..."

"Meant what, Bannon?"

She tried to speak, but whatever it was didn't rise to the surface.

"Sit down."

A low rumble of bodies rose as recruits shifted in their seats and sat erect. The former detective brought silence by speaking in a voice that demanded to be heard. "First lesson of the day. Most people know something about important events even if it's pure hearsay. It's your job to push through their desire not to reveal what they know. You determine what's important, not them."

Heather jotted a quick line in her notebook. Steve Smiley continued, "One more. The man behind Recruit Heather McBlythe. Stand up."

The chair behind her scraped. "Sir, Troy Franks, sir."

"Front and center, Franks."

Troy Franks drew to within a few feet of the man who commanded a bigger presence than his five-foot-ten-inch frame portrayed. Without asking, the former detective reached out and found Troy Franks' shoulder. His fingers slid down to

Franks' hand and then retraced the path back to the shoulder. He didn't stop. He felt Franks' neck, ran fingers along the crown of his head and did the same to his face.

When he had withdrawn his hand, Smiley announced, "Six foot two inches, approximately one hundred ninety-five pounds, Caucasian male, age twenty-five, scars over both eyes. Prior military. Most likely Army Special Forces. Bandage on shoulder indicates a recent tattoo or, more probable, the modification or removal of a tattoo. I suspect recently divorced, or in the process. No wedding band. The tattoo might be a woman's name. I also noticed he's sitting directly behind Heather McBlythe."

Smiley issued a wide grin. "Someone put the clues together for me. Is Franks interested in getting to know Heather McBlythe much better?"

A chorus of affirmative answers erupted.

Steve Smiley patted Franks on the shoulder. "Well? How'd I do, Franks?"

"A little too good, sir. Thanks for ruining my chances."

"I saved you time and aggravation. She's not interested in you." Without turning his head, he barked, "Are you, McBlythe?"

"Negative, sir." Heather cocked her head to one side. *How did he know that?*

"Have a seat, Franks. Okay, everyone, take out your notebooks and pens. Turn your chairs around and face the back wall." He waited until the noise died down before further instructions. "You have fifteen minutes to write down every observation and deduction you made of me. Whatever you do, don't turn around." He paused. "I'll know if you do."

2

Heather worked until Smiley said, "Time's up. Turn around."

Papers and chairs rustled.

"Look at your list and count how many things you observed about me by using sight. Write an 'S' at the top of the page and put the number."

He waited until the sound of pen to paper had ceased. "You should have at least twenty things recorded from sight alone. Less than twenty means you failed this exercise and you need to be more observant. A good habit to develop is start at the top of a person, their hair or the hat they're wearing, then work your way to the shoes or lack thereof. When I had my sight, I trained my mind to recall a minimum of forty distinct observations of every person I questioned." He lifted his chin and asked, "Did anyone get forty?"

Silence.

"Thirty-five?"

"Thirty-seven," said Heather.

"Not bad, McBlythe."

A mumbled "showoff" came from the back of the room.

Heather ignored the critic. Guys like him didn't last long.

Smiley continued, "Now add up every other characteristic you wrote down from sound, smell, taste, or touch. Put an OS at the top of your page for Other Senses and tally them up."

It didn't take long for nervous whispers to rise. "Did anyone have more Other Senses than they had Sight?"

No one responded.

"I wouldn't expect you to. Sight will be your number one asset. But, don't neglect your other senses.

"What you have so far are observations. I also asked you to make deductions about me based on those observations. My using a white cane is an observation. 'Steve Smiley is blind,' is a deduction you made from that observation. Write down the number of deductions you made about me."

It didn't take long before he asked, "Did anyone have more than seven things?"

"Yes, sir," said Heather.

"Anyone else?"

Silence.

"That's very good, McBlythe. Tell the class what you know about me based on your observations."

Heather took in a deep breath and began. "You're wearing a college class ring. At your age, which I judge to be just shy of fifty, I deduce you are a very proud graduate of your alma mater. Next, you're a dog owner. By the length and color of the hair on your pants, I'd say a golden retriever. You're very thrifty. I gauged this by the worn condition of your shoes, pants, and sport coat. Also, you needed a haircut two weeks ago. I didn't notice the smell of any cologne or aftershave, but I did notice a small amount of blood on your collar."

"And what did that tell you about me?"

"Two things. Your loss of vision occurred later in life and you're not fond of change. An electric razor would be more practical for you."

"Keep going."

"Your presence here tells me you miss being on the force."

"Anything else?"

"Your bearing is a little too slouchy to indicate a military background. You wear a wedding band, but your socks don't match. That, and the need of a haircut, tell me you're most likely a widower and you live alone. You have no desire for a new relationship and wear the ring as a guard against advances."

"Keep going. You're doing pretty good so far."

"There was one thing I found odd. You asked Recruit Bannon what she knew of the death of Ned Logan. That death hasn't been ruled a homicide yet. The lead story this morning was the murder of a cab driver. It received quite a bit of press coverage. The question I asked myself is why did you choose to question Ms. Bannon about the death of Ned Logan and not the cab driver?"

"And your deduction?" asked Steve.

Heather shrugged. "The death of Ned Logan is of particular interest to you."

"Excellent," said Steve. "Ned Logan was my college roommate. Anything else?"

"Yes, sir, but I think it best if I tell you in private."

"We all have our secrets, don't we, Ms. McBlythe? Very well. I'll see you after class."

He raised his voice. "Everything McBlythe said is accurate with the exception of my current ownership of a dog. He died five months ago. I haven't worn these slacks in nine months. Thus, Beauregard's hair remains on my trousers."

A voice piped up from the rear of the classroom. "What did you deduce from asking me my name?"

"Ahh, Hank Strother. I'll get to you in a few minutes. First, let me chat with Mary Bannon." He shifted to where he faced her. "Bannon, all it took was one sharp question and you turned to jelly. A series of quasi-accusations and I had you near tears. Here's what I deduced from our short conversation, Ms. Bannon. You have a fifty-fifty chance of graduation from this academy. Your chances of making it on the streets for more than a year are lower."

The room became graveyard quiet. Heather looked at the quivering jaw of the recruit. *Here it comes.*

"You have two choices, Mary Bannon: grow a backbone or find another line of work."

Pow. He nailed her.

A voice came from the back of the room. "You can't know that from one short conversation."

"Strother," said Smiley, his voice salted lightly with derision. "I thought I might hear back from you. I'm glad to see you're paying attention considering what you did last night."

"What do you mean?"

"When I passed your desk three strong odors assaulted me. The first, cologne. Old Spice, liberally applied. Breath mints came next, followed by last night's consumption of alcohol seeping through your skin. The Astros played last night. You spent an evening swilling beer at the ball park. Am I right?"

"I only had two beers."

Heather shook her head. *Wrong answer, Bozo.*

"Don't test my patience," snapped Smiley. "That 'two beers' fairytale won't cut it."

"You can't know where I was or how much I drank last night," challenged Strother.

Smiley raised his chin a little as his next words spilled out. Heather knew the signs. The red flag had been waved in front of the bull and it didn't matter that the bull couldn't see it.

"Strother, you have a voice like a megaphone and a mouth that needs a zipper. You were talking to the young man beside you about last night's game when I pretended to grope my way around the room. My suspicions of an alcohol-addled mind were further confirmed when you failed to stand before you gave your name and to address me as 'sir.' Add to that, you snickered when you heard a blind man was going to be teaching on observation skills. You mumbled a disparaging remark when Ms. McBlythe showed you up with the number of observations she'd recorded. You are not only a drunk, you're a belligerent and dangerous drunk."

"I still say you can't know where I was or what I was doing last night."

Steve lifted his hands upward in a sign of frustration. "You already stand convicted by your own words. Do you need more proof? All right. I'll be glad to give it to you."

"How?"

"The testimony of an eyewitness." Without waiting for a response, Smiley pointed with an outstretched finger. "The young man sitting in the last chair next to Strother, come up here."

A murmur of muffled voices rose and fell.

"Tommy Fletcher, sir."

"Tommy," began Smiley in a soft, fatherly voice. "You've been whispering back and forth with Hank since I arrived. You two are pretty good friends, aren't you?"

"Uh... good enough, sir."

He's baiting the trap.

"I'm going to ask you a series of questions. I warn you now not to lie or be evasive." He motioned with a tilt of his head. "Sergeant Holland is standing by the door, isn't he?"

"Yes, sir."

"He's listening to every word we say, isn't he?"

"Yes, sir."

"Lying to an instructor is cause for immediate dismissal, isn't it?"

"Yes, sir."

He's got a nibble.

"You went to the ball park last night, didn't you?"

"Yes, sir."

"You went with Hank, didn't you?"

"Yes, sir."

"You drank beer, didn't you?"

"Half a beer, sir. It got too warm for me."

"Hank drank the rest of it, didn't he?"

"Well..."

The voice of the instructor broke in with enough force to cause half the class to jump. "Tell him!"

Watch out, fishy.

"Yes, sir. Hank drank the rest of it."

"He got up every inning and bought a fresh beer, didn't he?"

"No, sir. He bought two at a time from the vendors who came down the aisle."

The hook is set. Now reel him in.

"My mistake," said Smiley. "One more question. Did Hank drive last night?"

The brief hesitation gave Heather the clue she needed to know the fate of Hank Strother. The delayed response mingled regret with conviction. "Yes, sir."

"Thank you, Mr. Fletcher. Have a seat."

The voice of the instructor came next. "Strother. Grab everything you brought to class and go to my office."

Fish landed, gutted, and filleted.

Heather looked on as the door closed with more force than necessary. Steve pointed again to Mary Bannon. "Bannon, was I too hard on Strother?"

"No, sir." The voice had more substance to it than her previous responses.

"Are you sure?"

"Yes, sir." Her words rang with conviction.

"Explain yourself."

"He's an alcoholic. He had at least seven and a half beers in a two-hour period. They stop serving in the seventh inning to cut down on drunk drivers. He was drunk when he drove home."

"You don't sound very sympathetic."

"I'm not."

"Congratulations, Ms. Bannon. Your chances of graduating and becoming a good cop are up forty percent."

His voice rose to address the entire class. "Train all your senses, not just sight. Ask questions, lots of them. Get over being shy about making people uncomfortable if you want to be a cop. This concludes my presentation."

Steve received accolades as recruits filed past on their way to lunch. The door shut and only Heather remained.

"Ah, Heather McBlythe, you didn't run out on me."

"No, sir. That was an impressive presentation."

The compliment passed with a simple nod. "Miss Bannon needed to find her backbone while Mr. Strother didn't belong." He paused. "You had something for me you didn't want to share with the class. What is it?"

"Before I tell you, I noticed you failed to pronounce your deductions concerning me. I'd be most interested to hear them."

"Are you sure?"

"That sounds ominous, but yes. Don't hold anything back."

"Very well. Your placement in the room intrigued me. You sat on the front row but against the far wall. This told me you were intent on getting the most out of the training but you wanted to remain inconspicuous, under the radar, so to speak. Next, I detected a slight accent in your voice. I had my suspicions when you gave only your name, but these were confirmed when you spoke later in complete sentences. Boston, I believe. You've done a good job in hiding your accent by purposefully slowing your speech and drawing out certain vowels, but that particular dialect is a tough one to shed."

"So far, so good," she said.

"A slight scent of perfume came to me. I can't remember the name, but I once splurged and bought Maggie a small bottle for her birthday. You, Miss McBlythe, have expensive taste."

"Keep going," she said.

"Based on the sound of your voice in relation to my ears, I'd say you're five foot six. I didn't detect any odor of makeup. Based on Troy Franks' interest in you, I'd say you're a naturally attractive woman of approximately thirty years of age."

"How did you come by my age?" asked Heather.

"Your skills in observation and deduction are too advanced for someone younger than that."

"I'm twenty-nine."

Steve acknowledged the one-year mistake with a slight bow.

"What else?"

"You're starting over. You've already been a detective somewhere. The cadence of your speech and the specificity of your words have 'detective' written all over them. No raw recruit ever comes up with over thirty-five observations, nor do any but a few regular cops."

"Any final deductions?"

"You're very well-educated and poised. I'm guessing Ivy League. For some reason things didn't end well for you when you were a detective. You have something to hide. Why else would you be starting over?"

She purposefully kept her voice flat and emotionless. "Most interesting. May I finish my observations and deductions concerning you?"

"By all means."

"You believe the death of Ned Logan will be ruled a homicide and you're trying to find a way to solve the case."

"Ned was on the university swim team and he stayed in good shape. The pool he drowned in is only about four-feet deep." He paused. "Sorry I interrupted. You were saying?"

Heather had to regather her thoughts. Her words came out slow but soon gained speed. "You were a superb detective and you're completely adrift without the job you loved. You believe these infrequent training classes are a form of charity from the department and you don't like that feeling. You also lost the only woman you ever loved."

Steve issued a tight-lipped smile. "If things don't work out for you here, look me up."

Heather lowered her voice and leaned in. "I might have to do that. Where do you live?"

"If you can't find me, McBlythe, I can't use you."

3

Steve Smiley swung open the door to his townhome and said, "That didn't take long. I went to the Academy on Friday and here you are on Tuesday. Were you followed?"

"No." Heather brushed past him and said, "It took a brisk walk, a ride on a bus, and an Uber driver with dreams of a NASCAR career, but I lost him. How did you know?"

"I guessed, but it was an educated guess. You being out of breath and the six insistent bangs on the door led me to believe—"

With hands tented on her hips, she interrupted. "Let's get something straight right now. Can you see, or are you really blind?"

"I can tell day from night, but that's all." He continued to speak as he ambled back to his recliner. "Dark, rainy days are a real pain. I'm not crazy about winter, either."

Steve settled himself in a recliner covered with a garish tartan plaid fabric and raised his feet with the pull of a wooden handle. She asked, "Do you know your recliner clashes with the okra-colored couch?"

"Looks fine to me," he replied. "Why don't you go ahead

and make a lap around the place? I know you want to check it out to see if it meets your need. It'll save you from making up an excuse to use the bathroom." He paused. "Correction: you also want to check me out, and you plan on doing that by giving the place a once-over. Help yourself."

"Thanks. But the need of a bathroom is no ruse. The tall mocha latte I drank on the bus was a mistake."

Steve pointed toward the hall. "First door on the right. Both bedrooms have full baths. Take your time looking around. If you're considering moving in you might as well know all there is to know."

"The shopping bags were too obvious. You must have heard the paper crinkle when I set them down."

"Bags instead of a suitcase. Smart, considering someone is tailing you. Of course, there's much more we need to discuss and clarify before we each reach a decision."

"Agreed."

Heather made her way through each room. She took in all she could and considered what it would be like living with a blind man who had a better idea of what surrounded him than most sighted people. The townhome appeared new, as did the beds, dressers, washer and dryer, furniture, everything. Blank walls. Only one photo adorned a nightstand in Smiley's bedroom. She picked it up and studied the face of a middle-age woman with kind eyes that held a dash of mischief. Her smile looked genuine, the kind that didn't have to be manufactured for a photo. She wore a skewed baseball cap over blond hair brushing her shoulders. In the photo the joy of Steve Smiley's life stood before an easel, one eye squinted, as if searching for the right perspective or blend of colors.

"So you're Maggie," said Heather in a whisper. "I think I would have liked you."

She continued through the townhome, opening every drawer, medicine cabinet, and closet. She even looked in the washer and dryer, searching everywhere she could to gather clues as to the character of this man named Steve Smiley. Experience had taught her people's possessions, especially what was hidden, give you a window into their lives.

Everything had a new smell to it. No trace of cigarettes, pipe, or, thank the Lord, her grandfather's cigars and the accompanying plumes of smoke forming a cloud around his gray head. A single, lonely bottle of beer stood in a near-empty refrigerator. The search revealed no hard liquor or wine and no collection of empty bottles in the trash. She repeated her floor-to-ceiling search of the kitchen, ending at a pitifully stocked pantry.

He spoke from the comfort of his chair. "Did it meet your approval?"

Heather settled herself on the couch. "Quite satisfactory, except for the pantry. You don't cook much, do you?"

"I'm big on calling Grub Hub." Smiley cleared his throat. "I'll go first. Then it will be your turn to bare your soul. Two years ago this past Saturday, Maggie... I take it you had a good look at Maggie's picture?"

"I did. Beautiful, with adventure in her eyes. You were a lucky man to have her."

Steve nodded an affirmation. "Anyway, Maggie and I were leaving an art exhibit at a small gallery near downtown Houston. We had to park some distance away. I was armed and didn't think anything about walking into a dimly-lit parking lot at night. Two homeless women and a man approached, seeking a hand-out. They were high as a kite, aggressive, and demanding. I never saw the second man. He took me out with the fat end of a broken pool cue. He then used it on Maggie. I lost my sight. Maggie died."

Steve leaned forward as if he were conducting an interrogation. "The cop in you wants to know if I'm seeking revenge."

"You read my mind."

"The answer is 'no.'" He settled back in his chair. "All four were caught and punished, if you can call it punishment. It's a story you've heard a thousand times. No reliable witness to identify them. That's one of the many disadvantages of being blind. I couldn't point at them and say, 'Yes, I recognize that one.' If they hadn't been caught with my gun and our cell phones they would have walked. As it was, all the D.A. could prove was possession of stolen property. They pled out to three years. Probated sentences, of course."

Indignation that comes from gross injustice rose up in Heather. It didn't happen often, but when it did her Scottish temper boiled like a cauldron. "Why don't you want real justice?"

Steve took in a deep breath and released it slowly through his nose. "Two reasons. The first is I'm getting it—slowly. A couple of years in the dark gives you plenty of time to think. Sure, I could arrange a hit on them, but would that bring Maggie back? Besides, like I said, justice is being doled out slowly. One of the women is already dead from an overdose. The guy who killed Maggie didn't last long on the streets. He's serving a sixty-year sentence for murder with a deadly weapon. His chances of being buried in the prison cemetery are good."

"What about the other two?"

Steve shrugged. "Remains to be seen. They sowed some bad seeds. I'm sure they'll reap a harvest sooner or later."

"And the second reason?" asked Heather.

"Simple. Maggie wouldn't want me to."

"If that's not why you want me, it must be because of Ned Logan."

For the first time since she'd arrived, Steve stiffened, his chin set as he spoke through clenched teeth. "Ned was murdered. I can feel it and see it. He was found at the bottom of his exercise pool."

"Do you mean an infinity pool?"

"No, an exercise pool. It's much smaller than a regular swimming pool. A steady stream of water pushes against the swimmer and they swim against the current. It's the same principle as walking on a treadmill. You can even adjust the current just like you can adjust the speed of a treadmill."

"What did you mean when you said you can see it?"

"Say the name 'Ned Logan.'"

She hesitated, but complied. "Ned Logan."

"I see pale red." He paused. "I don't really see it, but my mind gives me the impression I'm seeing through a red lens."

"I don't understand."

"It's called associative chromesthesia. Certain sounds evoke colors. I had it before I lost my sight. It's most common in highly creative people—artists, composers and the like. I'm none of those, but I'm pretty good at crime. Seeing red came in handy when we couldn't determine if a death was suicide or homicide. Leo and I would go to a crime scene and he'd say the name of the victim. I'd either see a shade of red or nothing."

"How do other people react when you tell them about this?"

"Most don't believe it. That's why Leo and I kept it quiet."

"Are you sure about Ned's death?"

"Pretty sure. I'll know for certain when we go to Ned's house. It helps for me to be in the place where the murder was committed."

"Any other superpowers?"

Once again, he morphed into a relaxed, rather dowdy widower. "That's it."

She shifted on the sofa. *Was this guy for real?* She'd have to check out this associative chromesthesia thing. He seemed to be waiting on her to continue so she asked, "Why is solving his murder so important to you?"

Even though they both knew he couldn't see her, he turned to face her all the same. "To begin with, Ned was a straight arrow, as fine a man as I've ever met. He was more than a friend, if you know what I mean."

"Yeah. I think I do." She paused. "What else?"

"Ned told me something a few years ago that I didn't pay much attention to at the time. He told me that if he died, he'd like for me to make sure his wife and kids were set up. I think I agreed to be executor of his estate. But he may have changed that because I haven't heard from Kate yet."

"Anything else?"

"Yeah. I went from wearing a gun and working twelve hours a day to sitting in the dark with nothing to do and nobody to do it with. If I don't get my mind and body in motion, I won't be around much longer. I've tasted the barrel of my .9 mm twice. What's the old saying? Third time's a charm?"

A pall settled over the room. To move the conversation forward Heather said, "I suppose it's my turn to tell you my deepest, darkest secrets. I'm sure you've concluded I come from a big pile of old Northeastern money."

"I gathered as much."

"Along with the money came certain... expectations. Chief among these was the completion of an Ivy League education —Princeton."

"Not Harvard?"

Heather breathed a sigh. "I needed to get out of Boston. Not all prisons have fences and bars."

"I understand. Please continue."

"After graduating, my father expected me to take a cutting off the money tree, water it with sixteen-hour days, fertilize it with my soul, and raise an orchard of little money trees to full maturity. I was to continue the time-honored tradition of the rich getting richer."

She expected a quip to come, but he only nodded.

"I was compliant in obtaining the education my father desired, but drew the line at Wall Street. Too many of my classmates became addicted to Aderall, cocaine, and greed. Some have already burned out." She paused. "Don't get me wrong. I have nothing against being rich. In fact, I prefer it. But, the relentless pursuit of *more* for the sake of *more* would be like slicing away bits of my soul until there was nothing left."

"What did your father say when you told him you wanted to become a cop?"

"He laughed. That is, he laughed at first. He thought it was a naïve girl's flight of fancy that would soon run its course."

"But you found police work to be to your liking, and that put you on a collision course with him."

"I pacified him temporarily by pursuing a law degree while I worked as a patrol cop. Father became concerned when I passed the bar and made sergeant a week later. I dug my heels in about being a cop and it resulted in quite a row. That's when he cut off my allowance. The transition from silver spoon to plastic fork took some doing, but I found I enjoyed the challenge of stretching a paycheck. When I received the promotion to detective, he became more determined."

"There's something you're not telling me," said Steve. "Your father turned up the heat even more by getting you fired from the Boston P.D. Now he's pulled strings all the way down in Houston and done something to get you removed from the Academy."

Heather leaned back on the couch and looked at the ceiling. "I underestimated his tenacity in tracking me and planting a false story. He seems to be intent on starving me into submission. He's gone so far as to hire people to track my movements to make sure I'll be dismissed from any job I happen to land." She let out a soft giggle. "It's all so silly of him. My grandparents on my mother's side left me an inheritance in a trust. On my thirtieth birthday I'll be obscenely wealthy."

"Your state of destitution is temporary?" asked Steve.

"Three months from now I'll be in a position to purchase this townhome complex and dozens more like it."

"But for three months, you need a place to live where you aren't known or bothered? Then you can reconcile with dear-old-Dad on your own terms. And your terms will include solving crimes."

Steve became silent for several long seconds. "It's doable. There are details, of course, but nothing that can't be overcome."

"Like what?"

"You need to disappear, to drop completely off the grid. No credit or debit cards, no checking account—you know the game as well as I do. The spare bedroom of a middle-age, blind ex-cop is a place nobody would look."

"So, you agree hiding here is a good plan? So far, we're on the same page."

Steve continued, "Considering your desperation, I don't think this next one will be a deal breaker."

Heather raised an eyebrow. "Hmm. Depends on what it is."

"Nothing unseemly, I can assure you. Maggie was my one and only." Steve cleared his throat. "However, we will need to change your appearance from time to time. Unless I'm mistaken, you're much too attractive not to notice. Luckily, that's easy to fix. You can make any gorgeous woman ugly, but doing the opposite is a lost cause."

"I think I can handle a little role play." Heather sighed. "I never thought I'd have to go into a self-imposed witness protection program."

"Do you own a car?" asked Steve.

"A Porsche."

"We'll have to get something else."

Heather stood and began to pace. "So, if you're just looking for a work partner, what are your expectations of me?"

Steve lowered his legs and cleared his throat. "I need your

eyes and a way to get around. You have exceptional powers of observation and you can drive."

Heather hesitated, but not for long. They might be mismatched roommates but both had needs, real needs, the other could meet. "So far I have no objections to this arrangement, but there are a couple of things on my end that might be a deal breaker."

"What are they?"

She dipped her head and lowered her voice to a whisper. "The first is money." Why was this so hard to say? She raised her chin and spoke up. "I'm down to my last hundred dollars. It took almost all I had to relocate. My father has been most effective in making sure I feel the pinch. I've been out of work for six months."

"That's no problem," said Steve. "I'll cover room and board and pay you enough to get you by until your ship comes in."

"One more thing. Max has to come with me."

Steve's head jerked back. "You didn't tell me you had a kid."

Heather laughed. "He's definitely my baby, but of the four-legged variety."

"A dog?"

"Not exactly. Max is a lazy, lovable lap cat."

Steve spoke through clenched teeth. "I hate cats."

Heather changed the subject before he could launch into a diatribe against cats. "When do we start going after Ned Logan's killer?"

Steve seemed to refocus and said, "So far they're calling it a suspicious death. The cops'll do some routine investigating but won't be real interested until after the autopsy. The coroner's always backed up. We should have about a week to wrap things up before we're told to butt out. I've already done some work, but we need to interview the family tomorrow. Can you move in today?"

4

Heather looked at her reflection in the bathroom mirror and frowned. A wig bearing a striking resemblance to the thatched roof of an English cottage, stiff and tawny, covered her mane of auburn hair. The makeup looked like cheap stucco. Globs of eyeliner and the longest, thickest, false eyelashes the store had to offer partially hid her emerald eyes. It reminded her of a brief flirtation with going Goth between terms at prep-school. She parted her lips and beheld teeth that bore a likeness to her hair, mottled dark-tan and yellow, something Van Gogh might have painted.

She backed away from the mirror and smoothed the front of a man's blazer, fresh from the garage sale she and Steve had attended at dawn's early light, her first garage sale ever. The navy blazer covered a dingy yellow shirt which buttoned on a side her fingers were unaccustomed to manipulating. She rolled her shoulders forward the way Steve had instructed. Sure enough, she seemed to shrink two inches and looked devoid of both ambition and a high school diploma.

"All I need is a dip of snuff and people won't know if I'm a man or a woman."

With her transformation complete, Heather prepared to make her grand entrance before a man who couldn't see her. She'd almost made it out of the bathroom when a voice boomed from the kitchen. "Heather! Get your cat out of here."

Oh no. What had Max done now? She took quick steps toward the site of Steve's explosion.

Her black Maine Coon squatted on the countertop, lapping milk from Steve's bowl of cereal. Max looked up as if to ask, "What?" He dropped his head and went back to lapping two percent from between squares of Frosted Mini-Wheats.

Steve's voice dripped with disgust. "I know people who owe me favors. They know people who do bad things. If your cat can't swim underwater, I suggest you do something with him."

Heather gathered Max in her arms and hustled him to her bedroom, stroking his head as she went. She sat him on the bed and thought about giving him a good talking to. He turned his backside to her, stretched, and lay down to clean his whiskers. She wondered if Steve was able to hear Max's sonorous purrs of contentment all the way in the kitchen.

By the time she returned to apologize, Steve had dumped the cereal down the garbage disposal. "Sorry," she offered.

He responded with a grunt.

"What time is Mrs. Logan expecting us?" She hoped to change the subject.

"Ten o'clock. I already told you that. Trying to get my mind off that sorry cat, aren't you?"

Heather shot back, "It's called redirecting. It's what you do when you have a hostile suspect or witness."

She could tell he tried not to, but the corners of Steve's mouth pulled up ever so slightly.

It must have been his turn to redirect because he asked, "Are you dressed like we discussed?"

She glanced down at her outfit. "Don't you think this is a little extreme?"

"All part of the plan. Kate Logan is a high-maintenance woman. She wants everything in her world to be perfect. Give her a big smile with those yellow teeth and watch her reaction. The way I have you pictured she'd count it a blessing if she didn't have to look at you very long. I'll keep her occupied and you snoop around."

"Anything special I'm supposed to be looking for?"

"Concentrate on her kids' rooms. One is out of college and on his own. The girl is a sophomore at Brown. You may not have a lot of time—"

"Brown? As in Ivy League Brown University in Rhode Island?"

"That's the one," said Steve. "I understand it's trendy for the *nouveau riche* to mix with you blue bloods."

Heather cringed as soon as she sat in the driver's seat. "Of all the cars in the world, why did you have to get a police auction Crown Vic? This ragged-out patrol car smells like a drunk tank."

"All part of your disguise and protection," said Steve. "The guys your dad hired to keep tabs on you are looking for your car, which is hidden under the canvas cover I had delivered. After you got booted out of the Academy, this is the last thing they'd expect you to drive. Besides, this car may look and smell a little gamey, but it has an almost-new police interceptor engine. It may not be able to outrun every car out there, but it can put the rental you said those guys are driving in the dust."

"Tell Leo thanks for keeping my father's minions occupied."

"He enjoyed it. It was no trouble considering the low-rent area you were living in. It made waiting an hour for a K-9 to sniff their car plausible."

Heather added, "And all the while they watched me pack my car. Detaining them in handcuffs was a nice touch."

"Leo loved it when you waved at them as you passed by." He paused. "Let's get going."

The trip passed without words. The rapid acceleration onto I-45 demonstrated the power of the car and brought back a flood of foot-to-the-floor memories in Boston. The sound of the wheels on pavement changed as they left the interstate. Being around Steve had made her more aware of sounds and smells. She pondered this as they followed a serpentine journey through The Woodlands, a migration destination for those fed up with Houston who had money enough to drive north until they encountered pine trees and less crime. Heather brought the car to a stop and said, "It's not a villa on the French Riviera, but this home is no slouch."

"Ned did quite well for himself after he left the D.A.'s office."

"Did he make a lot of enemies when he was an assistant district attorney? If so, this could get complicated."

Steve changed subjects, as she was learning he was apt to do. "I've been thinking how I want to play this. Ned, Kate, Maggie and I go all the way back to our first year in college. Ned and I stayed in touch, but I've only seen Kate a few times since he left the D.A.'s office. People change over time, but not Ned. Kate wanted to run with the country club set, not with me and Maggie. I'll need you to tell me what she looks like and give me your honest opinion of her. I'll also want a full description of the home."

"You got it, boss. Anything else?"

"Yeah. Make a bad impression on Kate and go do your snooping as soon as you can." He paused. "By the way, your name today is Pat Beerhalter."

Heather let out a snort. "With a name like that I don't see how I could make a good impression."

The opening of the front door produced a visual assault on Heather's eyes. Steve had warned her Kate Logan leaned toward glitter and gold, but she didn't know that applied to Kate's entire world. Even the area rugs, strategically placed on the gold-veined marble floors, set the stage for a Midas-touched mini-mansion. *New money and bad taste* sprang to her mind but, thank goodness, didn't escape her lips.

"Steve," gushed Kate. "How good of you to come see me." Kate swept them into her home with a motion of her hand reminiscent of a game show hostess. Steve had not come to *see* her. That was Heather's job. The *faux pas,* along with the attempt to slather her life in gold, set Heather's teeth on edge. She made a point of smiling widely and revealed a most unappealing set of incisors and bicuspids. Kate's eyes opened wide and then shifted to Steve, never to return to the lowly Pat Beerhalter.

"Hello, Kate. I'm so sorry to intrude on your time of mourning," said Steve. "Are you sure it's not too much of an imposition for me to come and offer my condolences?"

"Don't be silly. It's I who have been remiss. I do apologize for not reaching out to you when Maggie—"

Heather cut Kate off in mid-sentence. "You got a spot I can park Mr. Smiley?" Her Pat Beerhalter accent came straight from a single-wide trailer with a beer-can-infested yard, complete with a 1972 Monte Carlo, tires missing and up on blocks.

Kate Logan cringed from the tips of her highlighted hair down to her gold house slippers. She made a quick recovery. "Yes, of course. Let's go to the living room. Follow me."

Heather directed Steve to a wing-back chair, pulled out two pillows—gold, of course—threw them on the floor and said, "There you go, Mr. S. You look like a king on his throne." She turned and examined the room, but didn't look at the not-so-grieving widow.

"You got a TV I can watch?" asked Pat Beerhalter. "Mr. S said he didn't want me hanging around while he talked with you. I got a habit of flappin' my gums."

Kate Logan pointed toward a hallway. "The den is on the

other side of the hall bathroom. The remote is on the coffee table."

"Thanks, honey. Come get me when you and Mr. S are done chewin' the fat."

Heather slouched her way out of sight, then straightened her spine. She retrieved her cell phone, made a quick video of the den, and turned on the television, making sure to keep the volume loud enough to cover most any sound she might make. Her crepe-sole shoes squeaked on the marble floor so she left them by the coffee table and eased her way down the hall. Two closed doors were on her left and a third at the end of the hall. On her right stood another series of doors, all closed. With the kids' rooms as her main objective, she needed to hurry.

The first door on her left opened to a game room, complete with billiard table. The second smaller room contained a miniature beauty parlor with wash sink and all the necessary potions and lotions. At the end of the hallway, double solid doors opened to the master bedroom suite, an expanse of wall-to-wall gold carpet and baroque furniture. She made yet another video of the bedroom, bath, and closet.

Opening the first door on her retreat back to the den brought the corners of Heather's mouth upward. "Eureka," she whispered and scurried up a back stairway.

Upstairs might as well have been on a different planet. The carpet appeared worn and the doorjambs bore the marks and smudges of children growing into adults and fleeing the nest.

With the turn of a handle she entered the world of a young man, a singularly messy young man. It didn't take much of a detective to realize most of the lad's meals had been taken, and spilled, within these walls. The photos surrounding her showed a handsome high school boy involved in football and track. His two prom pictures showed two different girls, both with perfect teeth and afflicted with near-terminal cuteness.

She put her phone's camera to use again, scanning the room and the closet.

The next bedroom proved to be the polar opposite of the sty down the hall. A girl's room, no doubt, but a girl of order. Extreme order. The clothes in the closet looked to have been spaced with a micrometer. The toes of all the shoes and boots could have been set along a surveyor's line. Books on the shelves were arranged in descending order, a singular collection including *Gray's Anatomy* and more than a few relating to neurology, kinesiology, Alzheimer's, and dementia. Even the underwear and socks in closed drawers were folded and stacked with absolute precision.

Heather wanted to stay and examine everything in more detail, but the minutes ticked away. She didn't know how long Steve could make chit-chat and she certainly didn't want to get caught this far away from the TV's soap opera. She pivoted in the center of the room with her phone's camera capturing images as she spun a slow three-sixty. Easing the door shut she hastened to the stairway. In her rush to descend, a sock-clad foot flew out from under her. She landed on the bottom step with a resounding thud. No time to check for damage. She sprinted down the hall and into the den. She scaled the back of the couch and stretched her feet onto the coffee table.

Heather craned her neck to see Kate Logan as she entered the room and issued a tart, "Mr. Smiley is ready to leave."

Heather joined Steve, who had risen from his gold throne. He turned to the spot of the scuffing of Kate's house shoes and asked, "Do you mind if Ms. Beerhalter takes me to Ned's exercise pool? I don't plan on coming to the memorial service and it's the last place he was alive. I'd like to pay my respects there if you don't mind."

"Of course. Stay as long as you wish."

Kate pointed the way and Heather led Steve out a back door, past an outdoor pool, and into a glass-enclosed room between the main house and a two-story garage. Once inside Steve said, "Describe it to me."

Although there was no need to whisper, Heather spoke in a muted voice out of reverence for the man she knew only from Steve's description. "The exercise pool is halfway above ground. Bend over and touch it. You can walk all the way around it if you want to. It's not more than eight or nine feet long and the water is about four-feet deep, four and a half at the most. There's a pump at the front that forces water against the swimmer."

"It's not very wide, is it?" said Steve.

"Not more than five feet." Heather paused, then spoke in a normal voice. "Ned Logan."

Steve froze in place. "Bright red," he said. He hung his head for a moment and mouthed something she knew was not for her. After a near-silent prayer, he said, "Let's get out of here."

Heather reached in her jacket pocket and retrieved a glass vial. "Let me get that water sample you wanted."

Kate met them at the back door and led them through the living room and into the foyer. The front door opened before Heather could reach for the handle. A young woman wearing, of all things, a poodle skirt, saddle oxford shoes, a starched white blouse, and a pink bandanna passed through the portal and came to an abrupt halt. She tilted a cloth-side, wheeled suitcase upright and stared at the unlikely duo of strangers.

Kate made a shoes-to-hair examination of the girl and grimaced. "Carey, dear, please tell me you don't dress that way at Brown. I thought we agreed you'd not wear such garish costumes."

Carey rolled her eyes. "Mother," she said with chin raised, "who are these people?" Her voice held the sharp edge of suspicion.

"You remember your father's college roommate, don't you? This is Steve Smiley."

The young woman summoned a tight smile. "Of course. Please forgive me for not recognizing you. Father spoke of you frequently."

"How are you, Carey?" asked Steve. "I came to offer my condolences. Your mother tells me a memorial service will be tomorrow. I'm so sorry for your loss."

An awkward silence fell. Steve broke it by saying, "Goodbye, Katherine. Goodbye, Carey." He turned and said, "Are you ready to take me home, Pat?"

"Ready, willin', and able, Mr. S."

Three steps down the sidewalk Steve said, "You need to be more careful on stairways. That crash you made sounded like an elephant jumping off the high dive."

She came right back at him. "If you hadn't insisted I wear stretched-out socks, I wouldn't have slipped."

"Did you get a good look at Carey?"

"Yeah. Five foot four, one hundred and ten pounds. Straight black hair touching her shoulders. Obsessive-compulsive and unhappy in the extreme. Upper-middle-class girl wishing she were somewhere else doing something else."

"I guess you can spot 'em," said Steve.

"She's miserable. Carey was dressed like she's going to a sock-hop, not a wake, or whatever you do down here. She's in denial about her father's death, but there's more to it than that. That outfit she has on is a plea for help."

"What kind of help?"

"I'd say she's seeking attention, but what do I know? I studied finance and law."

"Don't sell yourself short. You know a lot more about twenty-year-old women than I do and you have great instincts."

"Thanks; same back at you."

Steve's cane tapped the side of the car. He made no move to get in. "I have a good camera with a telephoto lens. Everyone on my list will be at the memorial service tomorrow. Let's get close-ups."

Heather nodded and reached for the door handle. "Did I hear you call Kate 'Katherine?'"

"Yeah." Disappointment seasoned his words. "She goes by Katherine now."

"A gold-gilded name if I ever heard one."

"She's not the woman I once knew."

"Has she changed enough to be the killer?"

Steve took in a deep breath and released it in a huff. "I don't know. I can't rule her out. Let's go."

"Hold on a minute. A lawn maintenance truck is pulling into the driveway." A tall, slender man in his early thirties climbed out of a three-quarter-ton truck. She scanned the contents of the truck's bed: garden implements, bags of mulch, an orange five-gallon water cooler and a large ice chest. The lanky, dark-haired man walked to the side door of the home and entered without knocking.

"Now can we leave?" asked Steve.

"Yeah. Chinese for lunch?"

5

"Heather!"

Steve's summons came from his bedroom at daybreak. She threw back her covers and scurried to his room. "What? What's wrong?"

"Get your cat off my bed. Put him in your room and keep him there or I swear, I'll..."

Heather scooped up Max. "I told you I can't. If I close the door he'll tear up the carpet trying to get out. He has to have the run of the entire house. Besides, he likes you."

Steve sat up in bed, mumbling something under his breath. He slumped back and threw up an arm over his face.

She tried softening her voice. "Steve, I'm sor—"

"Don't! Don't say it."

Heather allowed an awkward amount of time to pass before her Boston accent and Scottish temper joined forces. "Get dressed, you grumpy old man. I'll cook you an omelet."

"Take Lucifer with you. We have a busy day ahead of us and it's off to a bad start."

After breakfast, Heather broke the silence. "How much did

you learn yesterday?" She rinsed the remains of an omelet from Steve's plate and placed it in the dishwasher.

"Some." He grimaced when he sipped the dregs of his coffee. "Kate had plenty of good things to say about her daughter, but virtually nothing about her son. She did drop the name Brittany Brown when I asked her who might have an axe to grind against Ned. She's an attorney—the only other attorney in Ned's office."

"Partner, or junior partner?"

"Neither. Kate thought that might be the problem. Brittany followed Ned when he left the D.A.'s office and she's right where she started. We'll pay her a visit in a day or two."

Heather filed away the name Brittany Brown. She reached for the coffee and poured Steve a second cup. He'd left his sunglasses on the nightstand and looked very different without them. More vulnerable. His thinning brown hair was a rat's nest. How she'd hate not being able to see, especially not knowing how her makeup looked.

Steve interrupted her musings. "Tell me your impressions of Kate."

"Do you want the unvarnished version?"

"Straight, no chaser," said Steve.

"If I only had one word to use, I'd say facade."

"Use more than one word."

Heather put down her coffee cup. "She's chasing her youth, but it's pulling away fast. She's had work done of the plastic variety. Everything that drooped or sagged has been pinned up, snipped or tucked. She needs to stop. There's a tipping point with plastic surgery when you begin to look freaky. She's got a way to go yet, but she's heading in that direction."

"What else?"

"She's obsessed with money and not happy that someone put her on a budget. I saw that in her home."

"Hmmm," said Steve. "Tell me about her home."

"Big and gaudy. Think of her design style as a mix between Louis XIV and a lottery winner. The intent is to show opulence, but everything is beginning to look dated. I'd say nothing new has been purchased in the last four to five years."

"Anything else?"

"Yeah. She has a boy-toy."

Steve had his coffee to his lips but immediately set it down. "Are you sure?"

"A pair of damp swim trunks, size thirty-two, on the rail of her oversize bathtub says yes. The men's pants, what few there were in the half-acre closet, were size thirty-six." Heather snapped her fingers. "I wonder if those swim trunks belong to the lawn maintenance guy. He's the right size and he seemed right at home. A nice-looking guy, in a swarthy kind of way. I'll check him out."

"It wouldn't surprise me if she did some daytime entertaining. Ned told me he moved into the apartment over the garage four years ago."

Steve took a sip of coffee and resettled his mug. "It's also possible she was spending money faster than Ned could haul it in. I bet she's set to get a bundle from life insurance and the sale of Ned's law practice."

"Kate told you that?"

"She all but said it. People obsessed with money like to talk about it."

Heather wagged her head. "Sounds like trouble in paradise. It could be motive enough to kill him."

"Yeah," said Steve as he raised his cup for another sip. He had pulled back into himself, another of his quirks.

Since Steve ended the conversation about Katherine, Heather moved on. "Was that Leo calling last night?" The question came to bring the turtle out of his shell.

Steve nodded. "He managed to find out there were two

superficial puncture wounds to Ned's back, about four inches apart."

Nothing came to her mind as to a possible cause, so she asked, "Any ideas?"

"I spent most of the night thinking about what could have caused the wounds. I think it was 3 a.m. when it came to me. Taser."

Heather envisioned the scene from the perspective of the killer. Someone stood at the side of the pool. Two metal wires snaked downward from a black and yellow, hand-held pistol-looking device. The wires led to barbed tips, like tiny straightened fishing hooks, which entered Ned's back and stayed there until he drowned and the killer yanked them out.

She spoke out loud, but mainly to herself. "He was killed the same way an electric eel would kill something that came close. Stun it and let it drown. Ned didn't stand up because he couldn't."

"That's how I see it... so to speak."

She brought herself back to the present. "What else did Leo say?"

"No signs of forced entry. Security cameras outside show the people that came and went all day. The Woodlands P.D. is concentrating on the two hours before and after the estimated time of death."

Heather thought for a moment. "How did the coroner determine that?"

"It wasn't a coroner," said Steve. "There were no obvious signs of trauma so the responding officers didn't suspect foul play. In Texas a Justice of the Peace is usually called if the death doesn't occur in a hospital. They give an official pronouncement of death and make a judgment as to the need for autopsy. If it hadn't been for the two small places on Ned's back, he might have gone straight to the funeral home."

"What's the time frame we're working with?"

"Ned's body was found at 11:45 a.m. Ned answered a call from his office at 8:15 a.m. Add fifteen minutes on each side and that's the four-hour window the cops are using."

"Are we getting a list of those people?"

"My former partner came through for us. Leo sent it this morning."

They both sipped their coffee and allowed the revelations to sink in. Heather broke the silence. "Are you sure you don't want to go with me to the memorial service? I could reprise my role as Pat Beerhalter."

"No. I'm not keen on funerals. Besides, a blind guy and Pat Beerhalter would only draw attention. I do want you to go, but as an upper-middle-class professional. Dress conservatively. Pull your hair back and wear dark glasses. Go late and sit in the back of the chapel. Leave before the last 'Amen' and park where you can get pictures."

Steve's plan made sense and she loathed the thought of dressing up as Pat Beerhalter again. A thought occurred to her. "Do you want me to talk to anyone?"

"Not unless something unusual happens or you have to. The internet search you did last night provided you with fairly recent photos of everyone. You should be able to recognize all of them."

"And you still want current photos?"

"Humor me. Old habits don't die easily. Expect the usual eulogies and a short sermon. Your mission is to get good photos and observe the actions of the people we talked about last night."

Heather thought for a moment. "That puke wagon you bought me to drive won't fit the image of a woman in heels and hose. Can I take my Porsche?"

"A black Camry rental will be here at nine thirty."

This guy doesn't miss much. "I'll go early and get a good place to park at the church. I might catch some of the people on the list as they arrive."

"Good thinking. Go get ready. You don't want to be late. And I'm expecting a delivery this morning. I'll need your help getting it set up this afternoon." He rubbed his hands together as if they needed a good wash. "With luck, you'll have the face of a killer looking at you tonight."

"It can't be that easy."

"Get pictures of everyone on the list and we'll go from there."

6

Heather's high heels clicked on the sidewalk as she approached her new residence. She knew Steve would be listening for the sound of her key scraping the lock on the front door. Her shoes came off as soon as she entered the townhome.

Steve spoke loud enough to be heard without turning around. "I'd think a debutante like you wouldn't have an aversion to high heels."

"I'm older, wiser, and hope to avoid the podiatrist's scalpel." She scanned the living room. Parts and pieces of something big awaited her arrival. "What bomb went off?"

"Quite a mess, isn't it? I got started unpacking, but didn't get far in assembly. I think the directions are over in front of the TV. If I'm not mistaken, Max is making sure they don't fly away."

"Cats love to lie on papers." She lifted her chin. "Is that pizza I smell?"

"In the oven, keeping warm. Salad's in the fridge. I've already eaten. You're later than I thought you'd be. Did everything go all right?"

"No problem, other than a long-winded preacher."

"Photos?"

"Everyone on the list except whoever fills out the bathing suit hanging on Kate's bathtub."

She retrieved a plate from the cabinet, pulled the pizza from the oven and mined the refrigerator for a salad. Over her shoulder she said, "You were right. Nothing unusual happened in the service, but I'm glad I went early. Kate and her son had a heated discussion in the church parking lot."

"Interesting," said Steve. "Did the family arrive together?"

"Kate came in a five-year-old Mercedes. Connor arrived early in an aging low-slung Audi and paced the parking lot until Mom arrived. She wasn't out of the car good before he was in her face. She threw up her hands and stormed inside with him nipping at her heels. Carey slid in just under the wire in a not-so-new Prius. She wore an appropriate black dress with all the right accoutrements. She looked nice."

She knew Steve had the scene in his mind by the slight nod. His pensive state changed with the speed of turning on a light switch.

"Heather," he snapped. "Your spawn of Satan is making laps around my legs."

"So? Reach down and pet him."

Steve lowered his voice and mumbled just loud enough to be heard. "I think he enjoys tormenting me. He knows I'm blind and can't hit him with the spray bottle. He's a sneaky little devil." His voice raised. "Do you put socks on him?"

"You didn't squirt him, did you?"

Steve reached for the water-filled plastic bottle with a pistol grip that sat on the table beside his chair. He pointed it in her direction and fired off two squirts. "Some people sleep with a pistol under their pillow in case of intruders. You should be glad all I have is a spray bottle. I'll teach him to stay off the kitchen counter and out of my bed."

The pizza, salad and a little time worked together to take the edge off Heather's anger at Steve's attitude toward Max. After all, it was his house and she'd sprung the news of her four-legged companion only after they'd decided it would be of mutual benefit for her to move in. All the same, she held out hope the two males would find common ground. She slipped into shorts and a t-shirt and strode back to the living room.

"Ready to get started?" asked Steve.

"It won't take long. There aren't many pieces." She busied herself assembling the legs and base to a cork board that measured six feet across and four feet tall. Twenty minutes later she admired her handiwork. "All done. What's next?"

"Pictures," said Steve. "Print them out and pin them spaced evenly apart running left to right across the top of the board. There's photo quality paper, push pins, and five-by-eight note cards on my computer desk."

"Old school, but effective," said Heather. "Keep everything in front of you. Sit back and let the brain grind out the answers."

"It's always worked for me," said Steve.

"Always?"

"No. But a lot more times than not. Give me detailed descriptions of each person and I'll be able to picture them as if I could see them."

It took a while to choose the best shots to print but, after a while, the last photo whirled out of the printer. She approached the cork board. "Any special order you want these in?"

"Family first, left to right, in birth order. Then the others."

"Top left," said Heather. "Kate, AKA Katherine, Logan." She pinned up Kate's picture. "Next to Kate is her argumentative son, Connor Logan. Beside Connor we have his Ivy League sister, Carey Logan. Next is Brittany Brown, the only other attorney in Ned's office."

Heather picked up another photo from a quickly-shrinking stack. "Mr. Brant Speedwell. Leo told you he discovered the body. There's a lot we don't know yet about Mr. Speedwell, but I got a good picture of him."

"Are you sure it's him?" asked Steve.

"Vanity license plate 'S P E E D' on a new Yukon."

"That may not be him."

"It is. I caught him at his SUV after the service. We went for a drink."

Steve's eyebrows shot upward. "And?"

"We need to keep him on the suspect list until I can check out some things."

"Like what?"

"Like things he didn't want to talk about with a complete stranger. I didn't push it. We traded phone numbers. He's most agreeable to another meeting."

"Be careful," said Steve.

Heather noted the concern in Steve's voice. It gave him an endearing quality, but she made a point to move on quickly. "Last, and possibly least, we have a blank space. We know Kate Logan is real chummy with someone with a size thirty-two waist, but we don't know who that is yet. It might be the yard guy, or it could be someone else."

Steve rose and walked to the board. He reached out with his hand and felt the slick surface of five photos and the uneven spot where a sixth photo would soon be placed. "Security cameras and initial police reports Leo scored for me show each of these persons on the property the day Ned died, except Brittany Brown. Almost all are within the four-hour time period police are using for the time of death."

Heather stood back from the board. "Who do I start with?"

Steve placed his hand on the second photo from the left. "You take Connor Logan." His hand skipped over Carey Logan's photo and rested on the next one. "I'll make an appointment to see Brittany Brown. I'll need you to take me, Ms. Beerhalter."

Heather rolled her eyes. "Any special way you want me to handle Connor?"

"He's a day trader. Perhaps you can put that finance degree from Princeton to good use. Can you handle it?"

Instead of answering the question she took hold of Steve's hand and placed it at the very bottom of Kate Logan's photo. "Kate Logan. Age fifty. Five-feet-five-inches tall. One hundred and forty-eight pounds after her last liposuction..."

She droned on, giving physical descriptions of each suspect down to the last mole and protruding nose hair.

7

The following morning, Steve had coffee brewing when Heather stumbled into the kitchen. She thought about the skimpy sleep attire she wore, but not for long. After all, what did it matter? In mid-stretch she asked, "What time is it?"

"It was five when I got up. About five-thirty now," said Steve.

"Good. I need to get going. I surfed the net and made phone calls last night, finding out what I could about Connor Logan. Every morning he works out at a gym not far from his apartment."

Steve brushed past her on his way to take a seat at the kitchen's bar. "What did you find out about him?"

She poured herself a cup of Costa Rican dark roast. "You told me he was a day trader. Ninety percent of the people who try to make money at that fail, Connor Logan included. Lately he's been trading penny stocks. The chance of success in that racket is even less."

"Ahh," said Steve. "What kind of man is he?"

"I tracked down some of his old high school friends and college fraternity brothers. By all accounts he's a decent guy. He made good grades in high school and was a good athlete, but that didn't transfer to college. A middle-of-the-pack student with a business degree. No mention of drugs other than a little pot a long time ago. He did the usual binge drinking in college but, by all accounts, is Mr. Moderation now. I got the impression he's likable, generous, and gullible."

"Is he hurting for money?"

"I'll find that out this morning." She carried her mug with her on the way to get dressed.

"Say, Heather."

She stopped and turned. "Yeah?"

"I don't mind you wearing that when it's only us two here, but make sure you put on a robe if we have company."

Her eyes flew wide open. "How do you know what I'm wearing?"

He faced straight ahead. She thought she detected a slight grin.

"I went through your dresser. You don't own any sleepwear that isn't sheer, sexy, and expensive."

Her temper flared. "You dirty old man. Who gave you the right to put your grubby paws all over my—"

"You went through mine," he countered. His grin spread wide. "How did you like my boxers? Pretty hot, aren't they?"

She stood speechless for several seconds and said, "You win this round, but it's only round one."

The gym's parking lot held a good smattering of cars, but Connor Logan's wasn't among them. All the better. The former police cruiser didn't match the image she wanted to portray. Today she'd be someone very much like her father wanted her to be. Besides, she could get inside and secure a one-day pass before he arrived.

Inside she received the grand tour, endured the sales pitch and issued a rather tart, "I'll see how today goes before I make a decision." Heather checked her reflection in the mirror and nodded approval. All of her curves were still in their youthful places. The spandex leggings showed off the contours of her legs, her torso discreetly covered by a sweatshirt emblazoned with Princeton University.

The front of the building, a bank of glass, gave a full view of the parking lot. She didn't have long to wait as, right on schedule, Connor arrived, made small talk with the receptionist, grabbed a towel, and headed for a forest of treadmills. He chose one three rows back from a television showing a business channel. Plugging in earphones, he punched in a program to the machine, then, off he went on a simulated run. Heather waited until he'd traversed a quarter mile, glanced at the program he'd selected on his treadmill and climbed onto the machine directly in front of him. Five minutes into her workout she removed the sweatshirt and tied the sleeves around her waist. She made sure the lettering of her university bounced in full view. She hoped the curves under her sleeveless skin-tight top would be bait enough for him to want to strike up a conversation when she finished her run.

Ending her run a few minutes before his, she flashed a friendly smile as she passed him and headed for the juice bar. It worked. The moth drew near the flame.

"Can I buy you a juice?" he asked.

She nodded and issued a coy smile. "Thanks. I left my debit card in the car."

Although much too young and way too eager for her, Connor Logan was, as his friends had described him, a nice-looking young man. His thick, blondish hair had a slight wave, his shoulders spread broad and he possessed a disarming dimpled smile.

"You're a long way from home," he said.

"I beg your pardon?"

"Your sweatshirt. Princeton."

She nodded. "Very observant."

He extended a hand. "Connor Logan."

His grip—firm. His smile—genuine. "Heather McBlythe. Pleased to meet you, Connor Logan." She made sure to flash a wide smile.

"What brings you to Texas?" he asked.

"Right now, a mile run and the number three kale-mango organic juice."

He reared back his head and laughed. "Right, first things first."

With orders placed he repeated the question.

"Business," said Heather. "I'm looking at acquisitions and investment possibilities in and around Houston." It wasn't a lie. The thought of her multi-million-dollar trust fund and what to do with it loomed on the horizon. "And you, Connor Logan? What are you into?"

"Trading stocks," he said with confidence.

"Day trading?"

"Uh-huh."

She lifted her eyebrows. "Penny stocks?"

"Yeah." His head tilted to one side. "How did you know?"

"You have that 'I-can't-wait-to-be-rich' look about you." The statement came out flat, as intended, neither a compliment nor a condemnation.

The drinks arrived and they moved to a pub-height table. While he took his first sip she asked, "Any hot tips on trades today?"

"As a matter of fact—"

Here it comes. The hot, can't-miss deal of the day.

His eyes widened. "A start-up company in Austin will announce development of a new game that's set to absolutely explode in time for Christmas. I've seen the data and all the results from beta test groups. Projections are for it to be one of the hottest sellers of all times. The press and all the big gamers who write blogs will be given access to the game at eleven a.m. central time. They'll play for an hour or two and hit their lap tops. By tonight, the stock should go up in value a thousand percent."

"Interesting. What's the name of this company?"

Connor's eyelids squinted enough for her to know his suspicion had been raised by her question. She offered a broad smile and patted his forearm that rested on the table. She looked him dead in the eye and said, "I know people who know more about penny stocks than you can imagine. Tell me the name of the company and I'll make a couple of phone calls. If this company is legit, then I won't invest until this afternoon. That gives you plenty of time to buy all the stock you want. I'll even stay with you until then, if you don't trust me."

Connor took a long pull on the straw, giving him time to consider. "Okay. You have an honest face and that Princeton sweatshirt tells me you might have some good connections. The company name is Yukyuk Graphics. Yukyuk.com is their website."

Heather grabbed her phone and scrolled through the directory. On the second ring she shifted in her chair. "Jerry... It's Heather. How're things on Wall Street?...Yeah? Three Adderall already today? Listen, I'm looking for some info. What's the word on a gaming company out of Austin called Yukyuk Graphics? There's a rumor they're going to make a big move today... Oh... Uh-huh... really? That's interesting. Thanks, Jerry. That's a big help."

She turned to Connor. "I want you to get on your phone and search a number for me. I already have it in my phone, but I want you to know I'm on the up-and-up. Get the number for the FBI, New York City."

His eyes grew wide but he complied. Once he had the main

number, she showed him her phone and the identical number he'd pulled up. She instructed him to put his phone on speaker and she'd do the talking. After working her way past two underlings a man answered. "Special Agent Tim Walker."

"Tim, it's Heather. Do you have time for a pump-and-dump on a penny stock that will take place today? I have most of the information you'll need."

"I don't have time, but I might be able to pawn it off on someone else. What do you have?"

"Two guys named Rothchild, working out of their basement in Minneapolis. Their company is called Yukyuk Graphics. Their dot-com goes by the same name. They're supposed to have a company in Austin, Texas that's hitting the market this afternoon with a can't-miss new video game."

"What's your source, Heather?"

"A day trader in The Woodlands, Texas named Connor Logan. He's with me now listening in."

"Mr. Logan, this is Special Agent Tim Walker. Can you go to our office in Houston this morning? We need to know who gave you the information to purchase stock in Yukyuk Graphics and any other information you might have about this scam."

Connor's posture became rigid. "Uh, yeah. I guess so."

"Good. I'll let them know you're coming. By the way, Mr. Logan, were you considering buying stock in this company today?"

"Well, yes. I was."

"You need to buy Heather dinner tonight. Whatever money you were going to invest would have been long gone by the time you sat down for salad."

Following some chitchat Heather said her farewells. "Nice guy. He works securities fraud. One of my Princeton buddies."

Connor sat dumbfounded, but managed to squeak out, "You saved my life."

"That's a little extreme, isn't it, Connor?"

"I went to one of those payday-loan places and gave them the title to my car. I was going to sink all the money I had and what I borrowed into Yukyuk Graphics." He washed his face with his hands. "The joke would have been on me. How can I thank you?"

"Get out of day trading. You're a nice guy, but you're a minnow swimming with sharks. Isn't there something else you can do?"

He gave a short nod. "I have a real estate license."

"Use it."

"That's what my dad said." His head hung for several seconds before he seemed to gather himself and said, "That FBI agent told me to buy you dinner. Can I?"

"I'm not sure that would be a good idea. You see, one of the properties I'm interested in acquiring is the building that houses your father's law practice."

Connor pulled back. "I didn't know he'd put it up for sale."

"He didn't." She gave him the look a mentor would give a student. "You've been involved in real estate. You know that successful agents get listings any way they can. They keep an eye out for unexpected life events. I do the same thing."

"Like deaths?" asked Connor.

"Deaths, divorces, sudden or severe illnesses, you name it."

"So your being here isn't a random meeting?"

"No. I went to your father's funeral and I knew you'd be here this morning."

A puzzled look came over his face. "But why did you keep me from losing my shirt on a worthless penny stock?"

The moment she'd worked for had arrived. She looked him straight in the eye. "Because I need information and I needed you to trust me."

"What kind of information?"

"If I'm going to sink money into an investment involving a multi-story commercial property which includes a law firm, I need to do a lot of due diligence. I've found that family members can be invaluable."

Her cards had been placed face up on the table. His response would tell if her plan had worked or not. She'd already found out what Steve wanted to know. Connor Logan needed money. It was her turn to do a little business of her own.

"I'm not sure how much help I can be."

She patted his hand. "I'll be the judge of that. First question. Was your father in any financial trouble?"

"Not that I know of. Things sort of fell apart four or five years ago between Mom and Dad. He put the whole family on a tight budget. Something must have changed last week. Dad told me his ship had sailed and would soon dock. He said things would be looking up quickly."

"Do you know what he meant?"

"Not a clue. Dad was a good lawyer. He kept secrets."

"Why were you down to a title loan on your car?"

"Dad cut me off. He wanted me to stay the course on selling real estate. He told me my odds were better in Vegas than being a day trader." Connor hung his head. "I guess he was right."

Heather didn't want to ask the next question, but knew she had to. "Were your parents considering divorce?"

The look on his face was one of hurt and uncertainty. "Dad wasn't. He always said Mom would come around and he wanted to be close by when she did."

"And your mom?"

He shrugged. "She's not dealt well with getting older."

"What can you tell me about your sister?"

His head tilted back and he laughed. "She's weird." He stopped smiling. "She's also brilliant and miserable."

With her back to the door, Heather didn't see the woman approach. A voice straight out of *Gone With the Wind* spoke in a molasses-covered accusation. "Connor Logan, I've warned you about strange women trying to pick you up in here." She ran a manicured hand down his cheek as her glacier stare fixed on Heather.

"Time for me to go," said Heather. She turned to the woman. "Give Aunt Pitty-Pat my best."

8

Heather winced as the worn-out tennis shoes squeaked with each step. As Pat Beerhalter she led Steve into the Logan Professional Building, a tan three-story brick edifice fronted by a parking lot loaded with newer vehicles. Other occupants of the building included a mortgage company on the bottom floor, and a title company and Speedwell Construction Company on the second floor. The Logan Law firm occupied the top floor, although it came nowhere near utilizing all the space.

As soon as the elevator door closed Heather turned to Steve and asked, "Did you know Speedwell Construction was in this building?"

"I remember Ned telling me the business office of a large construction company was here, but I didn't know which one. Has Mr. Speedwell called you back for the drink you teased him with?"

"Not yet. If I don't hear from him by tomorrow—"

The door opened on the second floor. Before she had a chance to finish her sentence, Brant Speedwell stood in front of her. She swallowed hard.

"Going down?" he asked.

She closed her gaping mouth and said, "No, hon. We're headin' up. I'll send 'er back down."

A snicker came from Steve as soon as the door closed. "I take it that was your second date with Brant Speedwell. You didn't get much information."

Heather's heart pounded. "Don't worry about me. Let's see how you do with Brittany Brown."

The name plate on the receptionist's desk read *Sunny LaForce*. When Steve and Heather entered, she had her back to them. Bending from the waist over a file cabinet, she showed the majority, and almost the minority, of long, tanned legs. She rose, turned and smiled. Her summer-blond hair framed a porcelain face, while a tight skirt started not a moment too soon. She proudly displayed her assets with shoulders thrown back.

Heather hoped her gasp didn't travel far. Before her stood the woman she'd seen earlier that day at the gym, the Dixie-chick with her talons deep into Connor Logan.

"How can I help y'all?" she asked with none of the water moccasin venom Heather had heard that morning. The accent and demeanor dripped of Georgia peaches, grits, and hand-held fans.

"Steve Smiley. I have an appointment with Ms. Brown." He paused. "And this is my aide, Pat Beerhalter."

Pat Beerhalter issued an extra-wide grungy smile which caused a mixed look of disgust and pity to flash across the face of the over-endowed, wannabe Southern belle.

"She's expecting you, Mr. Smiley. I'll tell her you're here."

The receptionist hung up the phone. "You can go right in. She's ready for you."

Heather led Steve to a chair in front of the attorney's desk and took a good look at the attorney. Brittany Brown appeared to be in her early forties, chunky, plain, and haggard. Her full, florid face and the fact that she poured her size eighteen body into a size sixteen dress telegraphed stress and discontentment. Heather wished she could tell Steve her observations, but those would come later.

Heather retreated to a club chair in the corner. An awkward silence was broken when Steve and Brittany Brown spoke at the same time. Nervous laughter followed with Steve saying, "Please, Ms. Brown, you first."

She laced her fingers together and rested her hands on a clear spot amid piles of folders. "I was going to say, it's nice to finally be able to put a face to your name."

"Oh? I wasn't aware you would know anything about me."

Her head tilted. "Oh, yes, I've heard stories about the world's greatest detective for years. You can't believe what a hero you were to Ned." Her voice dropped. "He counted you as the most trustworthy person he knew." She glanced out a window. "I wish he'd trusted me half as much."

"What do you mean?" asked Steve.

She took in a deep breath and let it out in a rush. "Ned kept a barrier up between us. He was a private man... almost secretive. I'm the only other attorney in this office. You'd think I'd know everything he was working on. That's not how it is—or should I say, that's not how it was."

It came as no surprise to Heather when Steve asked an open-ended question.

"How was it?"

A touch of pink rose in Brittany Brown's cheeks. "I'll tell you how it was. For the last two and a half years I've been slave labor around here, doing the same thing day in and day out." Her voice rose, as did the color in her cheeks. "Sixty and seventy-hour weeks were the norm. Nothing but one real estate sales contract after another."

"You must have been well compensated for your work," said Steve.

"Ha! That's a good one, Mr. Smiley. I'm on salary. The pay raises stopped four years ago." Something between anger and betrayal flashed in her red-rimmed eyes. "He made promises for years, but always vague ones. He said all I needed to do was stay the course a little while longer and he'd take care of me. He promised me a full partnership. He promised me... Oh, what does it matter what he promised? He's dead and you're in charge."

Steve stiffened. A jolt ran through Heather when she heard the phrase, "you're in charge."

"What do you mean, I'm in charge?"

"Don't be coy with me, Mr. Smiley," snapped the attorney. "You've read Ned's will."

"No. I haven't."

"I don't believe you, and I'm in no mood to put up with this."

Heather watched as Brittany Brown picked up a folder. She rounded her desk and threw it in Steve's lap where it slid off. She stormed out of the office, slamming the door as she went.

Heather stepped quickly to where Steve sat and scooped up the folder. "This will take me a few minutes to go through." She turned to the last page. "It's signed, witnessed, and notarized. It looks legit."

Heather sat in the leather office chair of the attorney and began to read. Eighteen minutes later, after rereading it, she announced, "Congratulations, Mr. Smiley. Ned Logan has named you executor of his estate and has given you authority to act *in loco pater familias*."

"I'm a little rusty on my Latin. What does that mean?"

"Simply stated, you are to act as the father of the family, the big cheese, the Exalted Potentate. The way this will is written, you control the purse strings until Connor Logan is thirty years old. After that, he takes over."

A long, low groan came from the blind former detective. "Do I have to wait that long?"

"No. Who gets what. and when, is totally up to you."

She allowed him to take it in for a moment. "Steve."

"Yeah." His voice couldn't have sounded flatter if he had been run over by a steamroller.

"You're in over your head."

"I know."

"I'll help if you want me to."

"Please. Where do we start?"

"Money. Always start with the money. You can't start divvying up anything until you know how much Ned had and what he owed."

"Good thinking."

"Steve."

"Yeah."

"This could get messy."

"It already is."

The ride back to Steve's townhome passed in absolute silence. Once there Steve slumped in his recliner, took off his sunglasses and rubbed his eyes. What could he be thinking? The term *pater familias* was as foreign to him as the dead language it came from. As for children, Steve and Maggie had settled that a long time ago. Careers and each other formed their small, but complete, circle of family. Now he found himself the unwilling, blind, stand-in father of a dysfunctional home. The middle-aged mother wished to be a vivacious, rich aristocrat who could turn back the clock and be thirty years of age in perpetuity. The son, good-natured but gullible, took risks and would likely hock the family jewels to bet on a three-legged horse in the Kentucky Derby. To top it off, there was the miserable, out-of-place daughter, twenty years old, bordering on an eating disorder and aptly described as "weird." What was

Steve to do with this trio? Assuming, of course, that one or any combination of the three, didn't kill the original *pater familias*.

The air in the apartment hung thick and stale. Or, maybe it was her imagination. Either way, Heather needed to get out and think—and if she did, how much more did Steve need to ponder his plight? "I'm going to grab some lunch and find a quiet place under a tree. Can I fix you something before I go?"

"No."

"Do you want me to bring you anything?"

"Yeah, pick me up a one-way plane ticket to the Bahamas."

Heather left Pat Beerhalter in a pile on her bedroom floor and down the drain of her bathroom sink. A tank top, black leggings, tennis shoes and a ponytail completed her reincarnation into Heather McBlythe. She pulled a lightweight hoodie over her head as she walked to the door. "I'll be back in a little while."

Steve grunted as she closed the door.

Her thoughts spun as she drove the blue and white cruiser to a neighborhood restaurant, grabbed a southwestern salad to-go and headed to a nearby park. The pine tree she settled under provided exactly what she desired: shade, quiet, and a gentle sway of the branches far above her head. Peace in the midst of an unexpected squall.

The salad looked awesome but proved to be a hot disappointment. The house dressing should have come with a warning label. Vinegar, cilantro and chunks of unnamed peppers from the Marquis de Sade's garden cauterized Heather's mouth. She set the plastic box aside and sipped a bottle of water.

As the burn subsided, a plan began to take shape. Money would be required. Lots of money, and it needed to come almost immediately. Steve didn't have that kind of money, and it was certainly more than the seventy-six dollars in her purse. But there was someone who had all she would need. She reached for her phone and selected a name she hadn't called in almost a year. A man's voice answered.

"Father... Heather. I have a business proposition for you."

Following the call, the breeze lost ambition. Heather's wayside picnic oasis became hot and sticky, what some people referred to as "close." The arrival of a squadron of mosquitoes hastened her departure all the more, but didn't dampen her spirits in the least. The conversation with her father had gone better than she expected. Much better.

Air-conditioned relief smacked her as soon as she opened the door to Steve's townhome. It appeared he had not moved a muscle, but a plate and scrunched napkin on the counter told a different story.

"How was the park?"

She considered the buoyancy in Steve's question unusual given how despondent he'd been only a few hours earlier. She matched the tone of her response to his. "Not bad until I was attacked by a flock of the blood-sucking hummingbirds you people call mosquitoes."

"Everything's bigger in Texas," he quipped.

She recognized the return of his droll sense of humor, a way of conversing that suited her down to the ground. "It sounds like you quit feeling sorry for yourself while I was away."

"For the most part. I dropped the 'e' from emotion and made a phone call or two."

Heather lifted Max from the couch cushion closest to Steve's chair and placed him on her lap. His purr combined entitlement with contentment. In many ways she and Max shared the moment. Steve had, in a very short time, righted his emotional ship, a good quality in a roommate. In addition, she'd taken a huge step in reconciling with her father. She had to admit, if only to herself, Max's purrs echoed her sentiments.

"Tell me more about what you've been doing," she said.

"I called Leo. The coroner officially ruled Ned's death a homicide."

"That means our suspects are going to be questioned by The Woodlands Police. That's going to put whoever's guilty on the defensive."

Steve affirmed what she said with a nod. "I was hoping we'd get to them first."

The pros and cons of the police interviewing the family and other suspects ran through Heather's mind. The cons far outpaced the pros. She continued stroking Max and asked, "Who else did you call?"

"Brittany Brown. We had a nice chat. She's wrapped around the axle."

"Sorry," said Heather. "I'm not up on all your homespun expressions yet. What exactly does that mean?"

"Wrapped around the axle? It means she's upset nine ways to Sunday, tied up in knots, beside herself with worry, and like a calf looking at a new gate. She's not quite to the point of squealing like a stuck pig, but she's sure got her knickers in a knot."

Heather shook her head and mumbled, "I'll never understand the affinity you people have for colloquialisms. Your passion for clichés rivals your love affair with chicken-fried anything. I take it you mean she's upset."

"To put it mildly. And by the way, you're set up to start going over Ned's books tomorrow morning."

"That sounds like a job for a CPA. Better yet, a CPA and a forensic accountant."

"You're right, but all I have is you. I hope you didn't sleep through your accounting classes at Princeton."

"What if I hire my own accountants?" asked Heather.

"On what I pay you?" He chuckled. "Knock yourself out."

Heather pressed on before he caught on. "While we're

talking about Ned's office, it appears Ned's secretary and Connor Logan are very chummy."

"Oh?"

"She didn't appreciate me talking to him at the gym this morning."

"Interesting," said Steve. "Describe her for me."

"I'm going to find a photo of her, put it on the board, and then describe her for you. There should be one on the fold-out of a back issue of *Playboy*."

Steve chuckled. "If you start putting up photos of every person you don't like, we'll have to get a bigger board."

Heather's cell phone jangled a ring tone. "Ah, Brant Speedwell. I was hoping he'd call." She swiped the screen. "Hello, Brant...Tonight? Sure. Where and when?... No, I don't know it. How 'bout I meet you at your office and we can go from there... Yeah, I know where it is...Sounds great...Yes, seven works for me."

Steve lowered his legs. "Someone has a hot date."

Heather put Max on the cushion beside her and walked to the kitchen. "It's more like prospecting for information than looking for a good time. However, he's not hard on the eyes." She opened the door to the refrigerator and looked at cold air and condiments.

Steve's voice found its way past the refrigerator's door. "Didn't you eat already?"

"The dressing on my salad was made of Napalm."

"That's too bad. I made tuna salad and ate every bite. I'm not sure what brand you picked up, but make sure to keep buying it. I've never had tuna so moist and I loved the extra-fishy taste."

Heather glanced down at the dish by Max's water bowl. A few mud-colored flakes remained. She looked in the trash and saw two empty cans on top. Purr-fect Delight Seafood Medley with the easy pull-top lid and albacore tuna packed in spring water, also with a pull-off top.

Uh-Oh. “Did you happen to feed Max?”

“He wouldn’t shut up until I did.”

“That’s nice. Thanks. Did Max enjoy his meal?”

“Yeah, he really went after it. You should have heard him smacking.”

I’ll never tell him. He’d squeal like a stuck pig.

9

The evening had not gone as Heather planned. The Irish pub, only a few blocks from the Logan Professional Building, proved to be a cacophony of noise, making discourse all but impossible. Brant shouted, "I'm sorry about the noise. If you'll give me another chance, I promise I'll pick a nice quiet place."

Once back in Brant's SUV she offered a full smile and said, "That made me long to visit Ireland again. In the pubs across the pond you're either standing cheek-to-jowl, being constantly jostled, or sitting on a narrow chair at an undersized table. The conversations are loud, salty and stimulating. It brought back nice memories." She reached over and rested a hand on his forearm. "You look tired... or is that worry I see in your wrinkled brow?"

"Both." He caught what he said and pursed his lips. As he turned into the parking lot of the Logan professional building he said, "I'm sorry. This wasn't a good idea." He shook his head. "That's not what I meant. It was a great idea, just bad timing."

Heather spotted a car in the near-empty parking lot. She reached in her purse, pulled out a dollar bill and handed it to

Brant. "Give this back to me, right now. You're hiring me as your attorney."

His baffled look came complete with pinched eyebrows. "Huh?"

She pointed. "In that car are two police detectives. They're here to question you about the death of Ned Logan."

"They already did. I told them all I know."

"I don't have time to explain." Heather's voice was all business. "If you don't want to take a ride in the back of their car tonight, you'll have to trust me. Give me the dollar back. I can advise you." She looked into gray eyes. "Ned's death has been ruled a homicide. You were the one who found him. That makes you a suspect. These guys aren't going to play nice. Do you understand?"

"Yeah, I guess so. I didn't know you were a lawyer."

"I am, but I'm not licensed to practice in this state yet. I'll be walking a fine line with what I say."

Two men met them on the sidewalk outside the front door. The taller of the two said, "Brant Speedwell?"

A nod of Brant's head took the place of words.

The man pulled back his coat revealing a pistol and badge on his belt. "Detectives Lowe and Hall from The Woodlands police. I need you to come with us."

"Why?" asked Heather.

The badge flasher scowled, obviously not used to his authority being questioned. "Who are you?" he asked.

Brant spoke before Heather could. "This is Heather McBlythe, my legal advisor."

The two detectives exchanged glances. Detective Lowe continued. "That doesn't change a thing. You're coming with us, Mr. Speedwell."

"Is he under arrest?" asked Heather.

No answer.

"Is he being detained? If so, what did you use to establish probable cause?"

No answer.

"Gentlemen, you may be used to bullying your way through interrogations. I'm not. If you wish to question my client, we're amenable, but it will be in his office." She pointed toward the door. "Shall we?"

Detective Lowe growled, but jerked the door open and the quartet made their way to the second floor. The two detectives sat across a conference table from Brant and Heather. Detective Lowe ground his molars while Hall, a thoughtful-looking man with milk-chocolate skin and close-cropped hair, took out a black notebook.

Heather wanted to keep them off balance. She needed them to ask many of the same questions she had planned to ask without them catching on to her real purpose. She'd be walking a tightrope. It had to look and sound good enough, but not too good.

Lowe proved to be the talker of the two. "Mr. Speedwell, before I begin, I need to read you..."

Heather interrupted. "Hold on a minute, Detective Lowe." She pulled out her cell phone, turned on the function that recorded audio and said, "April twenty-third, eight forty-five p.m. Parties present are Detectives Lowe and Hall of The Woodlands Police, Mr. Brant Speedwell, and Attorney Heather McBlythe. At this time I'm asking Detectives Lowe and Hall to produce their police identification and give their badge numbers."

"We've already shown you ID," snapped Lowe.

"That's not exactly true, is it?" countered Heather. "A glance at a badge on a belt is not an examination and Detective Hall did not go to that trouble."

Hall took his credentials out and passed it across the table. "Badge number 2971," he said in a soft voice.

Lowe tossed his and barked, "2613."

"Thank you, gentlemen. Before we begin I want it understood this is informal questioning. Mr. Speedwell has not been advised of his rights, and if he is, I will advise him to terminate this voluntary interview. He is prepared to answer all relevant questions honestly and to the best of his ability." She looked at Detective Hall, mostly to annoy Detective Lowe. "What is the purpose of your questioning Mr. Speedwell?"

Lowe slammed his palms on the table. "I'm the senior detective and I've had enough of this. I'll ask the questions and they're going to be directed to, and answered by, Mr. Speedwell, not some hot-shot lawyer. "

Heather returned his frozen gaze. "Please, Mr. Lowe. There's no need for raising your voice or acts of petulance. Ask your questions, and do so in a civilized manner. If you cannot, then I'll advise my client to invoke his Fifth Amendment rights and you'll leave here with no information. I'll also file a formal complaint against you and provide your superiors with a copy of this recording. It will then be up to you to explain why your rude behavior kept you from acquiring the information you seek. I already told you my client is willing to cooperate."

Detective Lowe took in a deep breath and hissed it out. "Mr. Speedwell, you found the body of Ned Logan?"

"That's correct."

"What time?"

"About eleven forty-five."

"Where did you find the body?"

"The bottom of his exercise pool, at his residence."

"What were you doing at his home?"

"I needed signatures on some real estate documents."

"Was Mr. Logan your attorney?"

"Yes." He looked at Heather. "He was one of my legal advisors."

"Was Mr. Logan your business partner?"

"Not exactly."

"What does 'not exactly' mean?"

"There was no formal partnership. Ned invested heavily in a real estate development I'm completing near Lake Conroe."

"How heavily?"

"A couple million dollars and a ton of legal work. It's a very large development."

"How much return on his investment did he realize before he was murdered?"

"Interest only, up to now."

"Isn't that a rather odd arrangement?"

"Ned trusted me to come through, and I will. I guess now it'll go to his wife, who will most likely blow it, but I'll pay it all the same."

"Or make it disappear?" asked Detective Hall.

The lone question caused Heather to shift her focus to the man who waited for just the right moment to pounce. She broke in. "Don't respond to that, Mr. Speedwell. You have no idea what Mrs. Logan will or won't do. Detective Hall is presupposing fiscal misconduct on your part."

"When are the repayments of principal and interest to begin?" asked Detective Hall.

"Interest has been ongoing. The first six months' principal and interest payments are already in an escrow account."

"How are the payments structured?"

"Eighty-three thousand, three hundred and thirty-three dollars a month for the next ten years."

Heather spoke up. "That's one million dollars a year for ten years."

Brant Speedwell issued her a nod.

She glanced at each detective. Detective Lowe appeared stunned by the amount while Hall remained poker-faced. "Are you finished with your questions?"

"Not quite," said Detective Lowe. He stared at Brant Speedwell. "Have you ever been arrested for a criminal offense?"

"Not as an adult."

"What about as a juvenile?"

Everything in her wanted to tell Brant not to answer. Except in rare cases, juvenile records are sealed. She wasn't fooled, but she needed to see how Brant would respond. She also knew the detectives were fishing for a reaction. They already knew the answer.

Brant hung his head. "I was arrested for involuntary manslaughter when I was fifteen."

"That involved a drowning also, didn't it?"

"It was an accident. The charges were dropped."

10

The next morning Heather pulled the cruiser into the driveway of the Logans' home. The air fresheners she'd attached to the air conditioner vents gave the car a smell that combined a nursing home, a pine forest, ocean breezes and a flower shop. Steve rode the whole way with his nose pinched. She glanced over at him. "Serves you right for buying this rust bucket and making me dress as Pat Beerhalter again."

He swung the door open and inhaled deeply. "Let's get inside before Holmes and Watson get here."

"Their names are Detectives Lowe and Hall. How much time do you think we have?"

Steve shrugged. "Kate didn't know for sure. They wanted her, Connor, and Carey all here first thing this morning. I'm hoping we can talk to each of them and be gone before they show up."

"Steve, our lawn maintenance guy is here again."

"What's he doing?"

"Unloading bags of mulch."

Steve stepped out of the car. "Can he hear me?"

"Not now. He carried a bag of mulch to the backyard."

“See if you can have a word with him before we leave.”

Heather scanned the street and peeked in the garage. “I don’t see Connor’s car. He may still be at the gym with Sunny LaForce.”

She placed Steve’s hand on her forearm and headed to the front door. Steve whispered, “Was that a hint of jealousy I heard in your voice when you said, ‘Sunny LaForce?’”

“Not jealousy. Wariness. I can’t get past the feeling that Connor is a lamb standing at the door of the shearer. Or worse, the butcher just took an order for lamb chops.”

Inside, Steve accepted Kate’s invitation to join her at the breakfast table for coffee. Heather begged off and made her way to the backyard, assuming the persona of Pat Beerhalter.

“Mornin’,” she said as she approached the lawn maintenance man. The name embroidered on his shirt read *Rance* and the company, *Done Right Landscaping*. He looked to be the kind of man a mother would warn her daughter to stay away from. Tall, dark, tanned, dressed in Wrangler jeans and a bicep-hugging shirt. He swaggered with too much confidence and had the ability to ignore without the least sign of regret, or beguile with charm if the occasion dictated. He took one look at gender-blended Pat Beerhalter and gave a dismissive nod.

Heather smiled to show off her yellowed teeth. “Doing a little compostin’ of the beds today?”

“Yeah.” He gave her a longer look. A cold look. “Who are you?”

“Name’s Pat. Pat Beerhalter. I’m the aide to Mr. Smiley. Do you know Mr. Smiley? He’s blind.”

He looked away and scattered mulch. “Don’t know him.”

“You must be Mr. Doneright of Done Right Landscaping. That’s a funny name. Ain’t never met anybody named Doneright.”

He made no attempt to correct her and turned to ensure his view didn’t include Pat Beerhalter.

Heather needed to turn up the heat. "Mr. Smiley is smart as a whip and a real good friend to Mrs. Logan. In fact, I overheard 'em sayin' he's the one that's going to be in charge of seein' who gets what and when from Mr. Logan's will."

Rance jerked upward, spun to face her and demanded, "What did you say?"

His reaction spoke louder than words. Eyes flashed with something akin to accusation. Rage couldn't be far behind.

"Oh, nothin'. I'd best be getting back to Mr. Smiley. He likes me to be handy when he has something important to do. Sometimes he has me read things for him. I had to read the will to him yesterday in the lawyer's office. Man-o-man, you shoulda' seen some of them words. I had to spell a bunch of 'em."

She turned and walked toward the house. The grin came as soon as she was sure Rance couldn't see her face.

Heather made it back inside and sat discreetly by an opening leading to the kitchen. She chose a place where she could hear Rance if he snuck in to eavesdrop but he couldn't see her unless he stepped into the living room. Steve and Kate had been joined by Connor, who slouched on the living room's gold loveseat still wearing running shorts and a tank top. Carey eased into the room and had to be prompted to sit near her mother.

Kate took a verbal swipe at each of her children before Steve could begin. "Connor, do sit up straight. And Carey, must you always dress like a refugee from a malt shop? You both knew we were expecting company this morning. Don't you care what people think?"

Connor straightened his posture while Carey rolled her eyes.

The faint sound of the opening and closing of the door that led to the laundry room brought Heather on point. The scuff of socks approached and stopped on the opposite side of the wall from where she sat.

"Thanks for agreeing to meet with me so early," began Steve. "Today will probably be a difficult day for each of you."

"Why do you say that?" asked Kate.

"The police will be here this morning to question you individually. If you haven't heard, Ned's death has been ruled a homicide. I know they already questioned you once, but this will be different. There are a very limited number of suspects. Unfortunately, each of you had the opportunity to commit the crime." He went on quickly. "I'm not saying any of you did, but you were all here during the window of time the police think it happened. You can't deny it and I'm advising you not to try. You each have already admitted to being at home or were filmed on the security cameras."

"How do you know about the security cameras?" asked Connor.

"I still have connections."

Kate asked, "What should we expect?"

Steve's voice conveyed a mix of concern and authority. "They've already determined each of you had the opportunity. What they're looking for now is means and motive. The most uncomfortable questions will deal with motive. They'll get personal, real personal."

Kate's eyes shifted left to right. "What do you advise us to do?"

"I'd like to talk to each of you one at a time. I'll ask you the same type of questions they will. I won't go easy on you because they're not going to. This way, you'll be prepared. There are two things you don't want to do. The first is lie. The second is allow them to put words in your mouth. Be as succinct as possible with your answers. Watch out for open-ended questions."

Carey came out of her shell long enough to ask, "What if one of us killed him?"

Steve's expression didn't change. "Get a lawyer. You're going to need a good one."

Before the first interview began, Heather rose and entered the kitchen. "Mr. Doneright, did you need something? Looking for a drink of water? That sure was nice of you to take off your boots so you didn't track up the floor."

His scowl could have melted tempered steel. "Yeah. I needed a drink of water." He turned on the heel of a white sock and made for the door.

Heather seated herself again in the same chair and waited for Steve to begin with Kate. It didn't take long before tissues piled up on her lap. Connor came next and held up surprisingly well under intense questioning.

Carey sat across from Steve with crossed arms and legs.

"Tell me about your relationship with your father," said Steve.

"What do you want to know?"

"Did you love him?"

"I guess."

"Did you hate him?"

"Sometimes." Her flat affect made her appear uncaring, cold, even disinterested.

"Why did you sometimes hate him?"

"I don't know."

"Yes, you do. You're a very bright young woman. More than bright–everyone says you're brilliant. Your dad told me your I.Q. is out of sight."

"So? I'm smart."

"Smart enough to murder your dad and get by with it?"

"If I wanted to."

"Did you want to?"

"Sometimes."

"Did you kill him?"

"No."

Carey had shown no sign of emotion that Heather could detect. Her posture remained relaxed but motionless, no movement of any facial muscles save the mouth to give answers and the occasional normal blinking of her eyes. She didn't fidget. There were no alterations in volume or inflection in her speech. Her responses might as well have come from a robot.

"We've come full circle," said Steve. "Why did you sometimes hate your father?"

A crack formed in the armor. She clasped her hands together and dipped her head. "He...he stopped being a dad."

Steve's voice softened. "When? When did he stop being a dad?"

The crack found its way to her voice. "About five years ago. Mom was going through some sort of weird woman thing and Dad didn't know what to do with her. He started working more and more. He worked like crazy. Mom had her first plastic surgery. Then, two more. Finally, Dad moved to the apartment over the garage."

"And that left you alone, didn't it?"

"Mom was sort of around, but she'd changed. She got a bunch of strange ideas about how my life was going to turn out."

Steve leaned forward. "Paint me a word picture of how your mom thinks your life should look."

Carey's voice reverted to a monotone. She stared out the window, apparently without interest in what she saw. "I'm to be Ivy League educated...married into an incredibly rich family... New York high-rise apartment...Broadway plays...summer in the Hamptons with trips to Martha's Vineyard and winter skiing in Aspen. And, of course, there are film festivals in Cannes and Telluride."

"Is she with you?"

Carey's next words came out jagged, each word enunciated crisply and separated. "Every–step–of–the–way."

"I see," said Steve. "Now paint me a word picture of how you want your world to look."

She glanced at him and returned her gaze out the window. "I'm a research chemist wearing a plain white lab coat. I'm in a small lab at the end of a long hallway. I'm doing important work. Work that will save lives. My hair is pulled back into a ponytail and I'm not wearing any makeup."

"What are you working on?"

"Alzheimer's–a cure."

"Why that disease?"

Carey continued to look out the window. A single tear slid down her cheek "When I was four, I saw what it did to Grandpa Logan."

Steve's next words sent a shiver of admiration down Heather's spine. "You want to be like your dad and bury yourself in work because, just like him, you're not happy and you don't know how to fix it."

A look of astonishment came across Carey's countenance. "I never thought about it like that."

"Do you think your dad abandoned you?"

She hesitated, her twenty-year-old's face contorted with a wrinkled brow and eyebrows pinched together. "I... I don't know. All I'm sure of right now is that I miss him."

"Thanks, Carey," said Steve. "We'll let ourselves out."

The unmarked car of Detectives Lowe and Hall pulled up to the curb as Heather backed down the driveway.

11

The tearing, shredding sounds of feline nails caused Steve to lift his chin. "What in the world is that cat tearing up now?"

"Nothing," said Heather. "He's sharpening his nails in a special box I got him. I'll bring it to you so you can feel."

Max finished his grooming with an immodest tongue-bath as Heather took his box across the living room for Steve's inspection by fingertips. His grunt of approval came as a surprise, but he didn't dwell long on his four-legged roommate's pedicure.

Rising to his feet, Steve went to the cork board. His hand moved to the picture of Connor Logan and traced an unseen line with his finger from Connor to the newly acquired photo of Sunny LaForce, the Dixie cupcake and receptionist at Logan Law Firm. "How long has Connor been seeing Ms. LaForce?"

"I don't know," said Heather. "Long enough for her to lay claim to him. Those baby-blues turned green with jealousy when she saw me talking to him at the gym. I wouldn't be surprised if she had a box like Max to sharpen her claws."

"Hmmm."

She guessed what would come next. If Steve had an assignment for her, he sometimes preceded his request with, "Hmmm."

"Connor owes you," said Steve. "You saved him the embarrassment of having to move back in with his mother after squandering every penny he had or could borrow. Give him a call and find out what you can about his relationship with the Scarlett O'Hara wannabe."

"Right now?"

"No time like the present. Put it on speaker so I can listen."

The phone rang twice before she heard, "Hello?"

"Hey, Connor. Heather McBlythe. I wanted to check up on you and see how everything went with the FBI."

"Great. They pumped out every drop of information I had in me and told me what a bullet I'd dodged. I can't tell you how grateful I am."

Max made a figure-eight path through Steve's legs while issuing a deep bass "purrrr." To her surprise, Steve made no attempt to kick him or even move. In her mind she issued her own, "Hmmm?"

"Listen, Connor, how about that dinner my buddy at the FBI suggested? My treat."

"Uh... uh... I don't think I can do that. You remember Sunny from the gym, don't you? Well... you see... it's like this, we're kind of getting serious, and—"

"Say no more. I don't want to do anything to get in the way of true love." She paused. "How long have you two been an item?"

"Not long. I knew her from Dad's office, but she pretty much ignored me until fairly recently. She started coming to the gym about four months ago and...what can I say? She's got it all and then some. That accent of hers is something else, isn't it?"

"It definitely is." Heather looked at Steve. His nod told her he'd heard enough. "I'll let you go, Connor." A thought ran through her mind. "By the way, have you given any more thought to going back into real estate?"

"I thought about it, but to tell you the truth, Sunny and I are considering other possibilities. It all depends on how much I get after Dad's will is probated."

Steve's expression of concern sealed her lips from the snarky comment that longed to escape. They both knew Connor's chances with a woman like Sunny to be somewhere between poor and none. She also knew Steve had new demands of parental responsibility weighing him down.

Steve's cell phone blowing up parted the weighty gray cloud hanging over him.

"Hello, Ms. Brown."

"How did you know it was me?"

"I have a phone with an app for blind people. It announces who's calling. Since it could only be you or Ms. LaForce calling from the Logan Law Firm, I knew I had a fifty-fifty chance. What can I do for you?"

"Please, call me Brittany. I need to apologize for the way I acted. There was no need for me to take out my frustration with Ned on you."

"I understand. Stress in these situations is high."

Brittany sighed. "Thank you for understanding. The other reason I'm calling is because I can't find the will I left for you to examine. Did you take it?"

"Yes. I brought it home to study."

Relief seasoned her next words. "Thank goodness. That's the original and the only other copy is on Ned's personal computer. He never told anyone his password." She paused. "I could have sworn he told me he kept a copy of the will in his personal file in his office."

"If you need the will, I can send it over to you. As for the password, Ned told me what it was several years ago. It's complicated enough I doubt anyone could ever hack it."

"I'll probably need the password, but not today. I was afraid something happened to the will last night."

Something about the last statement didn't sound right. Steve caught it too and asked, "Did something happen last night?"

"I think someone broke into Ned's office."

"What makes you think someone broke in?"

"I may be wrong, but you know how meticulous Ned kept everything. He couldn't stand anything out of place or the least bit messy, not even a sticky note on the outside of a file. I unlocked his office today looking for a copy of the will. It looked like someone had gone through his file cabinet. His personal file wasn't pushed down where you could read the label of the file behind it. That used to drive Ned up the wall." She paused. "Do you think I should call the police?"

"There's no cash missing?"

"No."

"Or anything else?"

"Not even a paperclip."

"Was Ned's personal file the only one that looked disturbed?"

"That's it, and nothing missing other than a copy of the will. Sunny said her files haven't been touched and she can't find anything missing either."

It didn't take Steve long to come up with an answer. "If someone was in Ned's office and they were good enough to get past all the security in the building, they were bound to be wearing gloves. The police aren't going to do anything but make a report if you're sure the only thing missing is a copy of a will. Call them if you want to, but I think you're wasting their time and yours."

"I'll follow your advice. When do you want to have the reading of the will?"

"Late tomorrow afternoon in your conference room. I'll send you a text with the names of everyone I want to have present."

12

Heather checked her email before she went to feed Max his morning breakfast. Steve, fully dressed except for shoes, sipped a cup of coffee at the bar as his sock-covered foot ran a path down Max's back. The cat arched up in a sign of much-deserved contentment. She couldn't help but smile. Max had done the impossible and won Steve over, one purr at a time.

"Where are we going for breakfast?" asked Steve, his voice buoyant and his hair neatly combed.

Heather regarded his appearance and concluded he cleaned up pretty darn good. "Wherever you want to go, but I'd better keep you away from middle-aged widows or divorcees. As handsome as you look, they might kidnap you and take you to Vegas for a quickie wedding."

"Are you trying to spoil a perfectly good day? That sounds like a nightmare involving a ball and chain."

"Speaking of," said Heather. "Did you think of something we might have missed last night? Any new thoughts or revelations come to you while Max and I snoozed away?"

"No. I think we covered everything during our marathon

session at the cork board. ” He chuckled. “You must sleep pretty deep. Max came visiting me about three a.m.”

“I must have been out of it. I didn’t hear him squawk when you shot him with your water bottle.”

“I held my fire last night.”

She shook her head and stood in wonder of how much Steve had changed. The case had brought out dimensions in him she didn’t know existed. “Grab your cane. I’m starving.”

Heather snatched her purse from the hook by the door. “By the way, Mr. Cat-Lover, I got the lab results back on the water from Ned’s exercise pool. Nothing unusual other than the salinity of the water wasn’t up to factory recommendations for a salt-water pool.”

He slipped on a pair of loafers. “That’s interesting.” Then he moved on to another subject. “I don’t care where we go, but let’s find a place that serves huge portions.”

Steve had no more stepped across the threshold when he jerked to the left. The crack of a rifle shot followed a half-second later. Grabbing his shoulders, Heather yanked him backward, sending them both crashing to the floor of the tile entry. She continued to drag him backward until she felt carpet.

“Steve! Are you hit?”

“My face.”

A jagged splinter of wood stuck out of his left eye, looking like a miniature jousting lance. “Don’t move and don’t touch your eye.” Blood trickled down his freshly-shaven face.

She scrambled to the door and kicked it shut. She punched 911 into her phone. “Shot fired. Pinewood Townhomes, number 604. One person injured. Roll EMS.” She crawled to the curtains and, ever so gently, pulled back a corner while repeating the message and giving other particulars to the operator. Nothing moved outside the townhome.

She examined Steve for further damage and found none. She moved to a different position. A longer look out the window revealed nothing but empty cars and vacant parking spaces. A ragged hole in the door frame, only inches from where Steve had been standing, gave witness to the seriousness of the event.

The trip to her bedroom took only seconds. She returned with her .9mm Sig Sauer in hand and squatted beside Steve. "I think someone else isn't crazy about you being the Logans' new daddy."

Sirens, ever-increasing in volume, approached. Five police cruisers, two unmarked cars, a fire department pumper truck, a second smaller fire department EMS response truck and an ambulance soon lined the parking lot of Steve's townhome. Skilled hands lifted Steve onto a gurney and off they went amid mechanical wails and staccato lights. Questions from patrolmen preceded similar ones from detectives. Redundant became too weak a word to describe what Heather endured.

"No, I didn't see who fired the shot."

"No, I didn't see anyone or a vehicle. But I did hear tires squeal, maybe a hundred yards away."

"No, I haven't seen anyone suspicious hanging around."

"Yes, he's a retired cop."

"Yes, he may have people who have a grudge against him."

"No, I don't know who. He was a cop. I was a cop. You're a cop. We all have people with grudges against us."

After an hour and a half she'd had enough. "Look, you've searched the house and you've checked our weapons to see if they've been recently fired. I'm telling you it was definitely a rifle shot. If you want to ask me anything else, I'll be at the hospital."

Heather expected to find a somber scene at the hospital. Instead, she stepped behind the curtain in the emergency room to find Steve and another man nearly doubled over in laughter. A bandage of white gauze, held in place with clear tape, covered Steve's left eye. He must have smelled her perfume or recognized her footsteps and he burst out laughing again.

"Heather," he muttered after he choked down his mirth, "Meet my old partner, Leo Villa. Leo, my new partner, Heather McBlythe."

Leo held his side and tried to get up. "Sorry," he muttered and slumped back down, his face an interesting shade of pinkish-brown and his body convulsing. After gaining control he rose and extended a hearty handshake. "We finally meet, Heather. Sorry about this sounding like frat night at a comedy club, but we got to talking about how stupid it was to try to shoot out the eye of a blind guy."

Steve erupted in another guffaw which caused Leo to bray like a mule. She could see the two in her mind's eye, fifteen years younger. The stakeouts they'd been on, the bond that had formed through shared experiences. Working together day after day had brought them closer than most people imagined possible. Once again they shared the bond that had been welded through time and trials, their reunion taking place in an emergency room, lubricated with gallows humor.

Heather moved to Steve's bedside and took his hand in hers. "What did the doc say?"

In as serious a tone as she had ever heard, Steve said, "The doctor thinks I'll lose my sight." Both men erupted again.

A voice came from behind Heather. "No, Steve's doctor said you need to take your two-man comedy show someplace else and make room for sick people."

A strawberry-blond woman nodded a greeting to Heather along with a wink. "If your name is Heather McBlythe then I understand you're the agent for these jokesters."

"Only one of them. I brought a clean shirt and his leash. Can I take him home?"

"Please do before people get the idea we don't inflict pain here. Speaking of pain, I gave him a local before I removed the splinter. Tylenol should be all he needs. Check the eye for the next three days for infection. Otherwise, he's all yours."

The doctor patted Steve on the leg. "Take care, Mr. Smiley. It's been real."

The doctor had no more left the area than Steve said, "Pancakes. We must have stacks of pancakes." He paused. "And new sunglasses. My old ones seem to have something wrong with one of the lenses. I can't see anything through it."

Again, Steve and Leo roared.

Relief swept over Heather as she handed a clean shirt to Leo for him to give to Steve. After Leo caught his breath he handed her the bloodied one that had been placed in a plastic bag. She stepped into an open space in time to see Detectives Lowe and Hall whoosh though the emergency room doors. Lowe approached with a scowl while Hall brought up the rear.

"Detectives," said Heather with a nod of greeting. "What can I do for you?"

"We aren't here to talk to you," snapped Lowe. "Is Steve Smiley behind that curtain?"

"He is. He's with another detective." She cocked her head. "Aren't you two a little far from home?"

"What business is that of yours?" said Lowe.

Doesn't this guy know you catch more flies with sugar? "Mr. Smiley is my client and he's been through a traumatic experience today. He and I have both been thoroughly interrogated. Do you have copies of the reports?"

"You know those haven't even been typed up yet."

Heather squared her shoulders. "Wait here a moment. I need to confer with my client and the detective interviewing him."

She stepped behind the curtain, put an index finger up to her lips so Leo could see not to talk or laugh. She whispered to Steve, "Shhh. I need to get rid of Holmes and Watson."

She stepped out and said, "Gentlemen, it will be at least

thirty more minutes before Mr. Smiley can speak with you. How about I give you a little money so you can get a cup of coffee in the hospital cafeteria?"

"Keep your money. We'll be back."

Heather waited until the duo cleared the emergency room before she said, "The coast is clear. Let's go get pancakes."

The curtain sped around a track in the ceiling. Leo stepped out and scanned the room. "They're not going to be happy when they find an empty bed."

She shrugged. "If Lowe weren't such a perfect hairball, I'd be nicer to him. Besides, all will be forgiven and forgotten later today."

Steve chuckled as he emerged.

13

The gray business suit with tiny, understated maroon pinstripes contrasted against a gleaming, white silk blouse, giving Heather the intended look of breeding, bearing, and success. Ankle-straining high heels lifted her to a height at eye level with most men. She'd applied makeup judiciously and with precision.

For his part, Steve had followed Heather's advice, donned the nicest suit in his closet, and covered the gauze bandage with an eyepatch. Not only did the black patch cover the injury, it gave him an air of mystery.

Heather's reflection in the mirrored walls of the elevator of The Logan Professional Building brought a nod of approval. She spoke in a matter-of-fact tone. "By the way, Steve, I'll be moving out next week."

"Oh... well... I knew you would sooner or later, but—"

"I'm buying the adjoining townhome. It's a mirror image of yours and, as you know, it shares a common wall. The only renovation we'll need to make is to put a pet door between the two dining rooms so Max can come and go as he pleases." She paused. Steve might as well have been made of petrified wood. “What’s the matter? Cat got your tongue?”

“There goes the neighborhood—a Yankee and an overweight cat.” He paused and choked out, “You didn’t have to do that, but thanks. Thanks a lot.”

Heather guided Steve into the reception area of the law offices at 5:37 p.m., exactly thirty-seven minutes late for the meeting they had scheduled for the reading of the will. Sunny LaForce had Connor so thoroughly occupied he didn’t respond to the door opening. He sat in her secretarial chair with his head leaned back. She dangled a chocolate-covered strawberry over his open mouth, bobbing it up and down like something on a hook, teasing with decadent bait in more ways than one.

Heather cleared her throat. Connor rose with a tinge of color rising up his neck and issued a meek, “Oh, hello.” The giggles and smile disappeared from Ms. LaForce’s face, replaced with a look of mild shock. This morphed into the solemnity of a nun, not an easy task considering how much of Sunny LaForce she’d put on display.

Heather took command. “Ms. LaForce, is everyone on the list present?”

“Yes.”

“I see you and Mr. Logan have availed yourself of the *petite repast* Mr. Smiley provided. Has everyone else had the opportunity to partake of the food and beverages?”

“We sure did,” said Connor. “I wasn’t expecting such a spread. Hey, what happened to you Mr. Smiley? Why the eye patch?”

Steve touched the covering of his injured eye. “Why don’t we all go into the conference room? That way I’ll only have to tell the story once.”

Heather’s cell phone signaled a text message. It read: *he sang, on our way up.*

As they entered the conference room she whispered to Steve, "The Mounties got their man to talk."

Steve nodded to indicate he understood the obtuse message. That's another thing she'd come to appreciate about Steve Smiley—he didn't need, or even like, life verbatim. He'd come from the shadowy world of hints and glimpses of incomplete puzzles. Solving people-puzzles made up his stock-in-trade, making one or more face appear from an assemblage of data, deductions, and a certain intangible known in the trade as 'gut instinct.' The time of revelation for this puzzle loomed large.

Heather glanced around the room. Those gathered had not been shy about partaking of either food or beverage. Almost everyone, with the exception of Carey Logan, held a stemmed glass of pinot noir. Brant Speedwell held a sweating bottle of dark ale.

She took Steve to a spot in front of drawn drapes and settled him in a chair facing the gathering of family and other interested parties. Chairs were placed on either side of Steve and she directed those gathered to arrange themselves so they would be seated, facing the trio.

"To be of aid to Mr. Smiley," began Heather, "I'd like Brittany Brown to join us in front. We'll be discussing legal matters of both a civil and criminal nature. Ms. Brown and I are both attorneys. Mr. Smiley has been named executor of the estate. Between the three of us, we should be able to answer all your questions."

Steve spoke up. "For my benefit, I'd like to arrange you in a particular order so I'll not be confused as to who is speaking. On the front row I'd like Connor Logan, Kate Logan, and then Carey Logan. Seated behind them I'd like Mr. Brant Speedwell and Ms. Sunny La Force."

Heather placed her hand on Steve's arm and whispered, "Lowe and Hall are here, too."

Steve announced, "We'll also be joined by Detectives Lowe and Hall from The Woodlands Police Department. The need for their presence will be made clear as the evening progresses."

"Detectives," said Heather. "I know you've had a full day and you must be starving. Please, help yourself to hors d'oeuvres. The evening promises to be lengthy and I dare say you're both famished."

The two looked at each other as if asking permission. Hall pursed his lips and nodded. Lowe needed no additional encouragement. The duo grazed with gusto, especially Lowe.

Steve listened until all became quiet and then cleared his throat. "When I heard Ned had died while swimming, I suspected foul play. I also determined to do what I could to bring his killer to justice. Through a series of fortuitous events, I've been aided in my quest by Ms. Heather McBlythe. She's a former detective herself, as well as an attorney and a graduate of Princeton with a degree in finance. Ms. McBlythe has been, and continues to be, invaluable. In addition, she must be a very convincing actress. Most of you have met her, either as she appears now, or as Pat Beerhalter, my dowdy aide."

Eyes squinted, trying to reconcile the incongruent images of Heather McBlythe and Pat Beerhalter. Heather said, "I apologize for the subterfuge, but everyone in this room was a suspect. As it turned out, each of you, with the exception of Detectives Lowe and Hall, of course, had a motive for killing Ned Logan. Everyone."

The repeat of 'everyone' brought about narrow-eyed glances of suspicion and looks of astonishment. The attendees scanned each other's face for any tell-tale signs of guilt. Heather studied the reactions. *Things are about to get interesting.*

Steve took over. He turned right. "Brittany Brown, attorney at law. Let's start with you. By your own lips we learned how years of devoted service at the Logan Law Firm resulted in nothing more tangible than Ned's word of better days to come. You demonstrated your anger to us in your office. You'd read the will and knew it contained nothing concrete that ensured you would ever be recompensed."

Brittany huffed, "If you're saying I had something to do with Ned's death, you'd better—"

Steve held up his hands as stop signs, slowed his pace and softened his tone. "You had motive. That's all I'm saying. What you didn't have was means or opportunity. You were here at the office, working away faithfully, like you've done for years."

"Then why all the theatrics?" asked Ms. Brown.

"I wanted to demonstrate how incriminating motive alone can be. Perhaps I should go through and list the motives of the others one-by-one?"

A chorus of denials rose from the gathering. Steve held up his hands again. "Quiet, please. I'll not air your dirty laundry, but every one of you either had something against Ned, or had the potential to benefit from his death."

Steve's voice rang with authority as Heather continued to scan faces. Most turned eyes downward and some of the expressions moved from denial to introspection.

"The next thing to consider is means," said Steve. "How was the crime committed? Here is where forensic evidence and other forms of evidence come into play." He took a long pause. "And this is where Ms. McBlythe and I ruled out each of you as a possible suspect. No one here murdered Ned Logan."

Kate Logan spoke the question that lined everyone's face. "If none of us killed Ned, who did?"

Steve rose to his feet. "I'll get to that in a moment. But first, I want to give you a good understanding of how we came to the conclusion that none of you killed Ned Logan. Let's replay the crime. We know Ned swam every morning in his saltwater exercise pool, a small pool, four feet by nine feet and only four feet deep. The current, generated by a motor, pushed him back as he stroked forward. While he swam, someone deployed a Taser. Stunned and incapacitated with an electric current, Ned drowned. Noticing the two small punctures on Ned's back, but not realizing their importance, the justice of the peace pronounced that Ned died under questionable circumstances. An estimated time of death was given as ten-thirty a.m., give or take two hours on either side. Therefore, the window of opportunity the police worked on was 8:30 a.m. until 12:30 p.m. That estimated time of death was incorrect."

Wide-eyed astonishment swept the room as Steve continued. "We also know, from Ms. LaForce's statement, that she spoke with Ned at 8:15 a.m. I've verified through the police that Ms. LaForce did place a call to Ned's phone at that time. Phone records verify the call lasted thirty seconds." He raised his chin. "Everyone following so far?"

Heads nodded. No one asked for further explanation. Steve continued, "I know this is painful for everyone to hear, but I want you to fully understand what really happened and how the estimated time of death is incorrect."

The eyes of the two detectives at the back of the room squinted as their focus sharpened.

Steve continued. "It's highly unusual for drowning victims to float. Forget what you've seen in the movies; bodies don't bob in a pool, at least not until a significant amount of time has passed. No, the bottom is where Mr. Speedwell should have found Ned and, by a sworn statement, that's where he was found."

Kate pulled a tissue from her purse and dabbed her eyes.

Steve had to have heard the muffled sob but carried on. "During our first visit to the Logan home I asked Ms. McBlythe to get a water sample from the pool. We sent it off to a lab for analysis and we have the results with us today. We'll turn these over to Detectives Lowe and Hall in a few minutes. I should mention that the forensic team of The Woodlands police also took a water sample on the day of Ned's death. The two samples proved to be almost identical in the salinity of the water." Steve lowered the volume of his voice a few decibels and the people leaned forward. "The autopsy report showed the salinity of the water in Ned's lungs to be significantly higher than the other two samples."

Eyes shifted back and forth as the gathering tried to come to grips with the importance of the saltiness of the water.

Steve pressed on. "One other fact needs to be made clear. Mr. Speedwell told police there were no motors running when he found Ned. Police reports confirm the breaker had been tripped. When Mr. Speedwell found Ned, he found him in stagnant water. That led us to two questions. First: Why would the murderer make sure the water didn't circulate?" Steve allowed the question to settle. "Second, why was the water in the pool less salty than the water in Ned's lungs?"

"Why is all this so important?" asked Connor.

Steve took in a deep breath and continued. "Hang on, Connor. We're almost there. Let's try to answer the question of the saltiness of the water first. What could cause the water in the pool to be less salty than the water in Ned's lungs?" The question again went unanswered so he continued on. "The obvious answer is the addition of water into the pool after Ned's death. But why would Ned's killer add water to the pool? That didn't make sense."

Steve rubbed his chin. "We then asked, 'What if the murder of Ned Logan was made to look like he died later than he actually did?' We know he sank to the bottom of the pool. We also know the pool's water wasn't circulating. What could have changed his body's temperature and decreased the salinity of the water?"

Carey Logan, looking straight ahead, said, "Ice."

"Thank you, Carey," said Steve. "You have the mind of a scientist. In a pool that size it wouldn't take a huge amount of ice to lower the water temperature, especially if the water wasn't being circulated. The cold water and the body both settled to the bottom. The time of death could easily be an hour or two before what was estimated. Eight to ten bags of ice would also explain the dilution of the salt in the water."

Connor Logan piped up. "But Sunny spoke to Dad at—"

Heather anticipated Steve's next question. She rose from her chair and stood beside him.

"Ms. LaForce," said Steve. "In light of what you've just heard, would you like to retract your statement concerning who answered the phone when you called Ned Logan's phone at eight fifteen?"

If looks could kill, Steve would have joined Maggie and Ned. Sunny crossed her arms and proclaimed, "Check the phone records. Check the cameras from this building. You'll see that I was here at the office and that I placed a call to Ned at eight fifteen, just like I said. You admitted it a while ago."

"Yes. You did indeed call Ned's phone, and someone answered, but it wasn't Ned. He couldn't. Dead men don't answer phones." Steve pointed in the direction of Sunny. "Remember, Ms. LaForce, I said no one in this room killed Ned Logan. I didn't say someone here was not complicit in his death."

Those attending had moved in their seats. Their gazes shifted from Steve to Sunny and stayed there.

"One more question, Ms. LaForce. How long have you known Rance Roberts?"

Connor Logan leaped to his feet. "That can't be. She and I are..."

His sentence died in mid-air as a malevolent smile pulled up one side of Sunny's top lip.

Steve spoke in a calm voice as he addressed the gathering.

"You might like to know why I'm wearing an eye patch tonight. It's because Rance Roberts, the lawn maintenance man for the Logan household and the co-conspirator of Ned Logan's murder, took a shot at me this morning. Luckily, he missed. All he managed to do was send a rather large splinter into my eye."

Gasps came from several, but the loudest from Kate Logan.

"Detective Lowe," said Steve. "Would you like to give us an update on Rance Roberts?"

"Glad to. Detective Hall and I took Rance Roberts into custody about three hours ago. We recovered a recently fired .243 rifle from behind the seat of his pickup. He tested positive for gunshot residue. Spring P.D. recovered the round he shot at you. We're sending it and the rifle for ballistics tests. We also recovered a five-gallon water cooler and a large ice chest from his truck. We'll be confirming Roberts' statement that Ms. LaForce made a large purchase of ice the morning of Mr. Logan's murder. We still have a lot of checking to do, but we've already established Rance Roberts and Sunny LaForce went on a cruise together six months ago."

The color drained from Sunny's face.

"Thank you, Detective Lowe," said Steve. "Before you escort Ms. LaForce to jail, I'd like to ask our two attorneys if they have any legal advice for her."

"I do," said Heather. "Honey, you're up to your push-up bra in trouble. You're not going to flirt your way out of this. For heaven's sake, give up the fake Georgia accent. It took me five minutes flat to learn you were born and raised in Baytown."

Heather looked to Brittany Brown, whose words seethed out. "Don't be looking for a final paycheck."

Handcuffs came out and a red-faced Sunny LaForce quoted three pages from *The Sailor's Handbook of Obscene Words and Phrases* before Detectives Lowe and Hall subdued and frog-marched her out the door. Connor Logan looked on, slack-jawed.

Brittany Brown stood and said, “Steve, Heather—you two know how to put on a show.”

Steve chuckled. “I wanted to waste a little time and give the detectives a chance to enjoy the food. And speaking of food and time, let’s take a break. Unless I miss my guess, all the glasses are empty and everyone could use a refill.”

14

Pages of the will made flapping, rustling sounds as people flipped to the next page at the same time. Brittany Brown concluded the reading of Ned Logan's last will and testament as the family members read along with their copies. Kate's eyebrows pushed together like someone squeezed her temples.

"This is all Greek to me. What was that term you used? *In Loco* something," said Kate.

"*In Loco Pater Familias,*" said Brittany. "It's Latin for 'in the place of the father,' or 'acting in the place of the father.' What it means is this: Ned handed all decision-making authority relating to his estate to Mr. Smiley. Steve is not only the executor of the will, but he has the legal authority to make any and all decisions concerning the estate until Connor reaches thirty years of age."

Kate sat erect, her posture as rigid as a block of granite. "How can that be? I was his wife."

"Not exactly," replied Heather.

A gaze like hot pokers bore into Heather. "What do you mean by that?"

"Ms. McBlythe is right," said Brittany Brown. "Technically, you and Ned legally separated four years ago. Ned did all the things he needed to do to make everything legal and binding so you would have no say-so on the disposition of the majority of monies or property in case his death preceded yours."

"I'll fight this," shouted Kate. "This isn't right. I... I'll—"

Heather interrupted with a simple, "No you won't."

"Yes, I will." Her nostrils flared.

Steve joined the fray with a firm, "No you won't, Kate. You won't have to." He paused and rose from his chair. "Before you or anyone else flies off the handle, I want you to listen carefully. I didn't ask for this, and I'm not happy about being in this position. I never wanted to be a father and I sure didn't want to be some sort of surrogate husband. But Ned chose me and he did so for a reason. That reason is he didn't trust any of you, with one possible exception. In your own way each of you kicked Ned out of your lives over four years ago. You may have pushed him out, but he remained faithful to each of you. If you'll be quiet and listen, you'll find out how faithful."

The tone of Steve's voice, the crisp articulation of his words, the rigid stance he took all displayed leadership. Heather scanned their faces. *He sure got their attention.*

"Good," said Steve. "Everyone's listening. The first thing I want to do is give you an idea of assets and liabilities. I've asked Ms. McBlythe to help me with this."

Heather stood as Steve settled back into his chair. "I've only had a chance to do a preliminary survey. Based on what I know so far, after debts and other liabilities are serviced, the estate of Ned Logan will be in excess of fifteen million dollars, not including the home, cars, and other miscellaneous items."

Kate gasped. Connor sat wide-eyed, while Carey took it in stride.

"It will interest you to know that ten million of the fifteen million comes from a real estate development deal Ned and Mr. Brant Speedwell were involved in. Mr. Speedwell's debt for legal services has been bought out by an unnamed investor. That ten million dollars is in the law firm's account, ready for dispersal at the pleasure of Mr. Smiley. Steve will now explain to you how he intends to distribute these funds."

All eyes shifted to Steve. "I'll start with Brittany Brown. Over the next twelve months you will receive payments amounting to one million dollars." Brittany's right hand went over her heart. "Ned Logan was a man of his word. He promised you'd be compensated for all the work you've done. In addition, I'm entering into an agreement to sell the Logan Law Firm. I have a cash offer in the seven-figure range. The only stipulation is that Ms. Brown is retained as a full partner."

Heather spoke next. "The figure of fifteen million dollars was mentioned a while ago. One million is going to Ms. Brown. That leaves nine million that will be going to the family. They will also receive an additional four million, the difference between what is owed on this building, the sale price of the building, and the purchase of the law firm."

Heather took her seat and whispered to a damp-eyed Brittany Brown, "Are you all right, partner?"

Her eyes widened and she whispered back, "You're buying everything?"

Heather smiled the smile of a cat finishing a bowl of half-and-half. "Who knew Pat Beerhalter had that kind of money? Actually, my father jumped at the chance to float me a loan when I ran the numbers by him and showed him the growth potential."

Steve turned. "If you two are finished, I'll get on with this."

"Sorry," said Heather.

Steve took in a big breath. Heather knew this would be the hardest part for him. He straightened his shoulders and said,

"There's fourteen million dollars on the table and I bet you're already thinking of ways to spend it. For at least two of you, that's the same problem Ned ran into. You have no trouble spending, but you don't want to earn it. That's why he structured the deal with Mr. Speedwell the way he did."

"What do you mean by that?" asked Kate.

Steve ignored her question and shot back with, "Kate, tell me, what does Carey want to do with her life?"

"Why...she wants to marry well and travel and... what business is that of yours?"

Steve shook his head. "You don't have a clue what she wants, do you Kate?" He shifted his head slightly. "Carey. I have fourteen million dollars to divide three ways. How much money do I have to give you?"

In less time than it takes to blink Carey said, "4.66 million. Actually the sixes reach to infinity, so someone will get an extra penny."

"What would you do with all that money?"

She didn't need to think. "Finish my undergraduate at Brown, then move on to a Masters and PhD at either Stanford or Harvard."

"Why those two schools?"

"They're cutting edge in Alzheimer's research."

"Excellent," said Steve. "I'll make sure you have all you need and give you a million dollars each time you complete a degree. You'll get the balance when you complete your doctorate."

"Now wait a minute," huffed Kate. "That's not what Carey and I agreed would be her future. She's to get her degree in public affairs, marry and settle down in New York, and—"

"Oh, Mother, please. Give it a rest. That's your dream, not mine."

Kate bristled. "It's all a moot point. There's no way you're getting into a prestigious master's program with your grades. You're doing good to scrape by now."

Carey had somehow matured five years with Steve's announcement of his intention to allow her to live her dream. She turned to her mother and spoke in an even voice. "You only know what I send you."

"What do you mean?"

"My degree will not be in public affairs. Chemistry has been my major since day one. I created official-looking forms and printed fake grade sheets to mail to you. The real grades went to Dad. He didn't like me deceiving you, but he understood why I had to." She looked down and smoothed her skirt. "Just like me wearing these silly poodle things. I'd never wear anything like this at Brown. I do it when I come home so you'll gripe about my wardrobe and not ask endless questions about what rich guy I'm going to hook so you can live your life through me." She kept looking down at an appliqued poodle on a chain. "Dad understood. He told me all about the ten million dollars that was going to start rolling in. He was so smart. He knew what Mr. Smiley would do."

Carey looked up at Steve. "Sorry I led you on with some of my answers, Mr. Smiley. I wasn't positive how you'd disperse the funds. I was so afraid Mom would get it all."

Kate's gaze shifted to the floor. She appeared to have been felled by a severe blow.

Steve swallowed hard and spoke through a cracked voice. "No harm, Carey." He cleared his throat. "Let's move on to Connor."

"Yeah," said Connor. "Let's do." Enthusiasm strained his vocal cords. Heather noted how quickly his broken heart had healed. It only took the promise of 4.6 million dollars to clear his mind of Sunny LaForce.

Steve turned to Heather. "Would you mind taking this one?"

"Glad to," said Heather as she stood and Steve took a seat. She gave Connor a tight-lipped smile and said, "Mr. Logan...

have you ever noticed how everyone calls you Connor and not Mr. Logan?"

"Huh? Well… no, I never noticed."

"Why do you think that is?" She didn't allow him to answer. "It's simple. You don't act like a Mr. Logan. You act like a Connor. Here you are, twenty-four-and-a-half years old and you're begging your mom for money, hocking your car to get a grub stake to invest in something that doesn't exist and mooning over a blonde-in-a-bottle whose dress didn't start soon enough, on the top or the bottom. Didn't you wonder why a few months ago she wouldn't give you the time of day and the next thing you know she's wanting to bed you and wed you, not necessarily in that order?" Again, she didn't give Connor a chance to respond. "By the way, Mr. Logan, she planned to be a young widow after she had your name on a marriage license."

"What do you mean?"

Heather tented her hands on her hips. "Don't you get it? The killing of your father was the first part of her plan. The second part was for her to offer you comfort while Rance Roberts did the same with your mother."

"Huh?"

"Turn the power on," shouted Heather. "Sunny LaForce had fifteen million reasons for killing your father. She planned to lead you by the nose, or some other piece of your anatomy, down the aisle and she'd be Mrs. Connor Logan. After that your mother would have a fatal accident. Then you'd be next in line."

"I… I can't believe she'd do something like that." His words had all the conviction of a shy middle school boy asking a girl to a school dance.

"She and Rance had already murdered once. What's two more?" Heather glanced at Kate. The color had drained from her face.

Heather shifted her gaze back to Connor. "Sweet Sunny had

you pegged as a naïve, reckless Cub Scout with money and gullibility coming out your ears."

The sweat on Connor's upper lip told Heather she'd gotten through to him. "Two words for you, Mr. Logan... grow up!"

Connor's Adam's apple bobbed up and down.

"To help you grow up, Mr. Smiley has devised a plan. I advised against it, but Steve's more trusting than I am." She paused. "Your father wanted you to work as a real estate agent. He did this because he saw in you exceptional people skills. You're handsome and engaging and there's an honest streak in you that's most admirable. The only things you lack are discipline, judgment and maturity. Working under the direction of a good broker, and in the company of professionals, will help you become a man your father would have been proud of."

Heather took a sharp turn with the conversation. "Mr. Logan, list for me the businesses in this building."

"Uh... a mortgage company on the first floor, a construction company and a title company on the second, and Dad's law office up here."

"With a lot of open space on the top floor," added Heather as she opened her arms wide. "Why do you think your dad never filled that space with other attorneys, or something else?"

"I never thought about it," he admitted.

"Well, start thinking. The only thing keeping this building from being one-stop-shopping is a top real estate sales team. Don't you see? Your dad was waiting for you to grow up and join him. Not in the same office, but on the same floor."

Connor's eyes darted back and forth as revelation of his father's love fell on him.

Heather kept going, mainly so she wouldn't get choked up. "With you or without you, this top floor will be renovated and a team of real estate professionals will be working here." She waited for Connor to look up. "Here's the deal. Mr. Smiley has $4.6 million to give to you on or before your thirtieth birthday.

If you want to do nothing until then, fine. You'll get a lump sum payment and you can blow it all. However, if you want to man up and go to work, he's prepared to pay you twenty-five dollars for every dollar you earn. Do the math. Earn a hundred grand in a year and get another $2.5 million. You'll have the entire amount long before you're thirty."

Connor set his jaw. For the first time Heather saw the man who was aching to get out. She sat down, emotionally worn out, but satisfied she'd done all she could.

Steve stood. "That only leaves you, Kate. I'll be blunt. I don't know what happened between you and Ned, and I don't want to know. All I know is Ned dropped the responsibility of taking care of you in my lap. If he were here, I'd ask him to stand still so I could take a poke at him."

"Me too," said Kate, but without malice in her voice. The revelations of the day, especially Carey's testimony of how clueless and self-centered she'd become, seemed to have softened and weighed Kate down at the same time. Connor finally crossing the threshold into manhood must have affected Kate in an equally profound way. She gave no objection to Steve calling her Kate instead of Katherine.

"What's my fate, Steve?" asked Kate.

"Work." The one word reply hung in the air like a Mylar balloon. "You'll have the same deal as Connor. Earn a dollar and you get twenty-five more. If you want to sell your house and get something more manageable, I'll give Connor all the money he needs to fix it up and tear out the exercise pool."

Kate looked up, her face registering doubt. "I've been out of the workplace a long time. I don't know what I can do."

Brittany spoke up. "You, Ned, and I set up this office a long time ago. You took care of all the secretarial duties and made it look easy. It just so happens I have a position that needs filling."

Heather added, "We'll need to start her with at least double what the last girl made. In fact, considering we'll be adding several attorneys and more clerical help, she'll probably need to be paid triple." Heather rose and placed a hand on Steve's shoulder. "And that doesn't include her having to put up with a grumpy private investigator who'll be sharing an office with his partner."

Jingle Bells, Rifle Shells

BOOK ONE

Jingle Bells, Jingle Bells...Rifle Shells?

Blind private investigator Steve Smiley and his partner hear a rifle shot. Hordes of Christmas shoppers scatter. A famous big-game hunter drops to the sidewalk. They grab the beautiful teen who was arguing with the man and flee to safety. The girl, the victim's adopted daughter, has one passionate request: find her birth parents.

Smiley and McBlythe's search intertwines with the murder investigation again and again—and uncovers a shocking secret. Like it or not, they must first identify the killer in order to discover the truth about the teen's adoption.

A host of suspects line up like Santa's reindeer. Can the determined investigators tie a ribbon on the case? Will this be the best Christmas ever—or will death and heartache be the only presents under the tree?

Scan above or go to
brucehammack.com/books/jingle-bells-rifle-shells/

From The Author

Thank you for reading *Exercise Is Murder*, the case that started it all for Smiley and McBlythe. I hope it kept you turning the pages to find out whodunit! If you loved it, please consider leaving a review at your favorite retailer, Bookbub or Goodreads. Your reviews help other readers discover their next great mystery!

To stay abreast of Smiley and McBlythe's latest adventure, and all my book news, join my Mystery Insiders community. As a thank you, I'll send you a reader exclusive Smiley and McBlythe mystery novella.

You can also follow me on Amazon, Bookbub and Goodreads to receive notification of my latest release.

Happy reading!

Bruce

Scan above or go to brucehammack.com/the-smiley-and-mcblythe-mysteries-reader-gift/

About the Author

Drawing from his extensive background in criminal justice, Bruce Hammack writes contemporary, clean read detective and crime mysteries. He is the author of the Smiley and McBlythe Mystery series, the Star of Justice series, the Fen Maguire Mysteries and the Detective Steve Smiley Mysteries. Having lived in eighteen cities around the world, he now lives in the Texas hill country with his wife of thirty-plus years.

Follow Bruce on Bookbub and Goodreads for the latest new release info and recommendations. Learn more at brucehammack.com.

Made in the USA
Middletown, DE
24 February 2025